THE BLUEBELL'S MYSTERY

BY
Francis Goodman

© 2006 Francis Goodman

All rights reserved. No part of this publication may be reproduced in any form or by any means – graphic, electronic, or mechanical, including photocopying, recording, taping or information storage and retrieval systems – without the prior written permission of the author.

ISBN: 1-905451-28-8

A CIP catalogue for this book is available from the National Library.

This book was published in cooperation with
Choice Publishing & Book Services Ltd, Ireland
Tel: 041 9841551 Email: info@choicepublishing.ie
www.choicepublishing.ie

Dedication

In thanks to my family for their help and support and in particular a special thanks to my wife for her inspiration.

Chapter 1

The smoke sneaked towards the sky. It was doing its best not to let anyone know where it had come from... a thatched whitewashed cottage set in the curve of the river on a carpet of green. This was home to James O'Shea, his wife Rose, two daughters Cathleen and Mary, sons Tom and Peter.

The quietness of the morning was shattered by the noise of the police making their way towards the O'Shea house. This scene was being watched from the high side of the valley by Tom the oldest son.

He realised his family were going to be harassed and felt sorry that he was not going to be there to treat these pro-British thugs to a few thumps. He had stopped at the high side of the valley to look down and admire the flower of the blackthorn. It was as though it had snowed only on the hedges, creating an eye catching view down and across to the far side, it was breathtaking. The white-hedged fields, with their different shades of green were beautiful. Seeing the police made Tom move quickly. The cattle he and his brother Peter had stolen from one of the landlord's estates had to be hidden. He considered these people a plague on the face of the earth and thought it strange that he should stop at this time and spot them. Did god have something to do with this, he wondered?

The banging on the door and the shout: 'This is the police,' woke everyone. 'Get out here now or we'll burn the house down.'

Pulling his jumper over his shoulders, James O'Shea opened the door in a hurry to be told, in a sneery arrogant fashion:

'You people, are involved in cattle stealing. We've been told all about it, now tell everyone to get outside quickly.'

'You know as well as I do that's a lie,' shouted James, with as much arrogance as the policeman, although he was wondering who the informer could be.
'According to our source of information Mr.O'Shea you're the one telling lies. Now hurry and get everyone out of the house.' The sergeant looked annoyed.
Mary and her sister Cathleen dashed out in a panic wearing only their nightdresses. They had a shawl and a cardigan thrown over their shoulders, trying to cover themselves properly. They thought the house was on fire. Not being fully covered they soon felt the chill of the morning air, even though the sun was trying its best to bring a little warmth. The young policemen were thrilled to see the girls skimpily dressed this was what they wanted.
'Do you have any weapons on you?' asked the sergeant; it was a ploy to search the girls.
'No we don't,' shouted James in a matter of fact way.
'Search them anyway,' said one of the policemen, in his self-important way.
He felt that working for the British they could do what they liked to the Irish. In an anxious manner one of the young peelers walked towards Mary with a grin on his face. When he was about to put his hands on her, she threw her arms out to push him away shouting loudly, 'Get away from me you cheeky brat.'
When Peter saw this he lashed out with a thump and caught him on the nose. He fell back but his friend began to beat Peter with a whip, James caught this fellow with a kick in the groin, he could see the pain on his face.
'How dare you try to put your hands on me,' shouted Cathleen, giving her abuser a nasty slap. He backed away quickly, with a stinging red jaw.
She glanced at the sergeant. He caught her eye and he thought she looked pretty. He'd try to get to know her better but now was not the time. She wondered why was he looking at her. Maybe he fancies me but he

works for the British. What a pity she thought, he does look handsome.

'Back off lads,' the sergeant called, seeing that these people were not taking any abuse.

'Mr.O'Shea, we came here to check how many cattle you have and to see how many are stolen.' James could see the smirk on his face.

"I'll show you what cattle I have, all two of them.' He pointed down towards the river.

'Look there, those animals belong to me and you can tell your idiot informer to stop telling you lies. Now go away and leave me and my family alone. Sometimes we have cattle here belonging to John Curtis and other farmers. They leave them here a few days before the market. We wouldn't know who owns them until the farmer himself arrives to collect them.'

'That's a right load of rubbish.' The sergeant roared at him. 'Why the hell do they leave their animals here?'

'Because they don't want to walk the fat off them on the day of the market.'

The sergeant pointed his finger at James and said: 'We'll be keeping an eye on you and the rest of your cattle stealing friends. This is not the last you'll hear from us do you hear that,' he sounded wicked.

'We're heading off now to see your neighbour Mr.Curtis. The two of you and your friends are stealing cattle and we know it. It's only a matter of time before you're caught and then you'll lose your homes and farms.'

James watched them go and wondered would Tom get the cattle hidden in time. He hoped that John Curtis wouldn't get into trouble. He had helped the O'Shea's when they were in arrears with rent years earlier.

Mary, Cathleen and their mother went inside, shocked and crying. Cathleen in a laughing crying voice said: 'Did you see that feckin' idiot trying to put his hands on me Mary? I gave him a right smack. I'll tell you, I wiped the smile off his face quick.'

Mary could hear the quiver in her voice.

'Didn't Peter give that smart guard a good thump on the nose?'
'Yes he did and the brat deserved it. They don't give a damn about stolen cattle, they were just here to harass us. They're a shower of perverts.'
'You two stop calling those policemen names and let's get the fire lit,' their mother shouted. 'It's chilly this morning.' They could see she was upset.
'We'll make ourselves a drop of tea,' said Cathleen.
After a while things settled, they sat around the fire and watched the draught from the chimney make the wooden embers shiver, smelt the smoke, and felt the heat gently soothe the body. They relaxed and talked. Mary now at sixteen years of age looked at Cathleen saying. 'Are father and the boys stealing cattle like the police said?' She saw the look Cathleen gave her mother.
'Yes, I thought you knew that Mary.'
'I was suspicious but I want to know for certain!'
Her mother interrupted saying: 'Well we've been able to scrape by with a decent sort of a living due to the poteen making. We cultivate the garden and the boys do a bit of cattle stealing with their friends.'
'It's a dangerous sort of thing to be messing around at isn't it?'
'Don't worry Mary, all the farmers are in on it, but don't talk about it, because you can't trust anybody.'
With a relaxed movement of her hand she pointed to the can in the corner and said: 'Mary do me a favour will you? Take that can and go down to the field and see if you can get some mushrooms. It will take your mind off this carry on anyway.'
Cathleen jumped up, picked up the can, grabbed Mary by the hand and said: 'Come on let's go, sure we might be lucky and get a full can this time.'
'I'm going down to the well for water girls and I'll check to see if there are any eggs. Maybe I'll find the nest that stupid hen is trying to hide from me.'

The girls could see that their mother was showing the strain of police harassment and the stress of all the years of struggling. Her slightly bent body looked frail as she walked down the garden. The grey hairs of time could be seen mixed with her black hair of youth. Mary could see that age was starting to steal her energy as she walked towards the well.

Tom thought the police might come as far as John Curtis's farm so he made sure the cattle were long gone.

'I'm going out to the garden to do a bit of digging John.'

'That's great Tom it needs looking after.'

Picking up the spade, Tom said. 'I'm expecting to see the police here soon.'

'Do you think they'll bother coming this far?'

'Indeed they will.'

He wasn't surprised when he heard the trap and its occupants coming up the lane, and pulling up close.

'Who the hell are you?' he heard a voice from behind. He looked round to see the sergeant.

'Who the hell is asking?' said Tom smiling, noticing the sergeant was upset by his reply. He must not have got a good welcome at home he thought, delighted.

'Don't you get smart with me. I'm a sergeant in the police and if I don't get a proper answer, you my boy will get a hiding.'

He signalled his men to be ready to give Tom a hammering. Two of them headed towards Tom who stood with the spade in his hand, ready to defend himself. He recognised one of them as Mr. McCoy who worked on the Dunaghy Estate as a game warden, he was a nasty man. He'd heard stories about him doing terrible things like having men beaten and taking more of their land as payment in rent for the landlord.

'I'm Tom O'Shea.'

'That's better, where's Mr. Curtis?'

'He's in the house. Anything you want to know I'll tell you because I look after the place for him.'

'I'm here to check how many stolen cattle he's got.'
'He has four cows out there in that field.'
Tom pointed outwards with his hand. 'Look, drag your arse up there and ask them if they're stolen. I'm sure they'll tell you anything you want to know.' he started laughing.
He saw the look on the sergeant's face he wasn't impressed at all. Tom didn't catch the nod he gave his men, but he did feel the thump on the cheek and the kick on the leg. Another blow on the face and his nose was bleeding. He was booted several times in the thigh as he lay on the ground.
'You don't get smart with me you thief,' he was warned.
The spade was thrown out of his reach, and he knew that the best thing to do now was to take his beating say nothing and wait for another day, because there were too many of them. The two animals he had brought here were safely hidden.
After checking the cattle, the sergeant shouted at Tom.
'We're here because we've been told that you and some of your neighbours are stealing sheep, cattle and grain.'
'You're going to hear that sort of thing anyway, people just like to be talking,' Tom said as he wiped the blood from his nose.
'Stop stealing do you hear,' said Sergeant Farrell in a low and what seemed a concerned fashion, leaving Tom wondering about him.
'I'll get to the bottom of this racket do you hear.'
He then walked over to the house, a thatched-white washed cottage with two small windows and a half-door. Looking inside he saw John Curtis sitting in a high-backed chair reading a book. To his left a staircase rose to a loft, no doubt his bedroom. The sunlight shining through the window created a shadowy glimmer over the room. He noticed the fireplace was made from limestone, a pillar on each side with a flat piece of timber across the top. The heavy black smoke going up the chimney told him the

fire was not long lit; there was a pot sitting on the swing rail over the fire, presumably spuds for the dinner.

'Hello Mr. Curtis, my name is Patrick Farrell. I'm a sergeant in Her Majesty's police force,' he said with a smile on his face. As John stood to walk towards him, Mr. Farrell noticed his slow walk and his hunched back. He could see that time and trouble had taken their toll on this man's body.

John looked at him with an inquiring look.

'So your name is Farrell? That's a strange one and you're in the police force.' He was surprised to hear this.

'Your grandfather wouldn't by any chance have lived down at Loughegish?'

'Where my grandfather came from is not the issue here. We heard you're stealing cattle and everything else.'

'Have a word with Tom O'Shea. He works here, he's in the garden. What you're saying is not true anyway.'

'We already did have a word with your man and I think he understands quite well what I'm talking about. We're leaving now but no doubt the carry on of you lot will bring us back again.'

John wondered was he, being warned by a friend or was this man just talking nonsense. He'd have a word with James O'Shea about this Patrick Farrell.

He watched as the sergeant and his henchmen left and wondered was he related to the police chief who had arrested his son.

It was years ago after the Famine when he was younger and stronger. He and some of his friends were involved in a row with a few peelers who had come to his house to collect rent. These men were harassing him and his wife. Luckily enough his son Michael and a friend Seamus, who were both strong supporters for the cause of Irish freedom, arrived home. A row started between the peelers and the young men. One of the policemen was badly beaten. Two weeks later the police

saw Michael and his friend at the market. 'Look who's here Seamus, I think we're in trouble,' said Michael.
A policeman came up to them and said: 'You two men are under arrest for assaulting one of my officers.'
They were taken to the barracks for questioning and were given a terrible beating. They protested their innocence by telling the sergeant that they were only defending themselves, from police harassment.
'You are being held here until a judge arrives in a few days time and then you can plead all the innocence you like,' said a policeman.
'You'd better get them seen to by the doctor or they won't be alive then,' said another guard sneerily.
As they were being transported from the barracks to the doctor's, their escort was ambushed. When the guards reported back to the barracks that the prisoners had escaped, they were reprimanded. Sergeant Byrne told them. 'We'll leave it for now and we'll surprise our Mr. Curtis and his son in a few days.'
They did pay him a visit some weeks later to no avail. When John received word from America, he knew he'd never see his son again. For this he blamed the English and rightly so. This was the reason he got involved in cattle stealing and poteen making. He'd spend the rest of his life trying to thwart the British at every turn. Within a few years of his son escaping to America, his wife passed away. After having struggled through the years of the Famine, now he was alone. Luckily, with the help of his neighbour James O'Shea and his family, he managed to fight the hunger. People were still finding it hard to live. This was Ireland, a very poor and troubled country, in the 1860's.

Chapter 2

Timothy Melen was seventeen years of age. He was attending college in London where he was studying civil engineering. He'd have to attend school for another year and a half, then he would be out and free with plans to change the world engineering wise.

Although the weather was wild and wet, it was warm and comfortable in the coach. The journey took him through many villages where he felt he could improve on the local architectural standards.

He was travelling to the docks to sail for Ireland and home. The weather was so bad he'd have to stay over for a night or two. He'd have a few drinks and enjoy himself if he could. After all, he was on his own and no one would know. He'd sailed from this port many times before and knew his way around the dock area. His ship the "Terenca" was going to sail tonight or whenever the weather allowed.

He was born in Ireland and spent his school years going back and forth to England. His home was a castle in Ireland that had been built about two hundred years before his family moved there. He remembered his younger years spent at home and the things that frightened him, especially the silvery man who stood in the hall. He had a big sword and shield sitting on the wall beside him. He imagined if he annoyed him too much he'd pick up the sword and cut his head off. He could laugh now at the imagination of a child of four or five. He enjoyed the days when he and his brother Fred would hide from each other and at times get lost on the pathways that were darkened by the overhang of the trees. The eerie silence and quietness of these lonely places was frightening. His dreaming on his way to Liverpool shortened the journey.

Timothy saw the ships out in the bay. There were no sails in view and the weather was wild. Out along the seafront the waves were rolling in as if they were trying to wreck anything and everything along the sea wall. He felt a bit of its anger in the coldness of the breeze when he stepped from the coach. It was the month of November and when the sea got wicked it had the water, the cold and the misery of it all, to throw at everybody. He headed for the nearest tavern to secure a place to stay. The girl at the counter looked attractive.
Timothy's 'Hello,' was met with a smile.
'Can I help you?' she said.
'Is it possible to stay here for the night?'
'Do you think you will stay only one night?'
'That depends on the weather and boy it's bad out there.'
'May I ask where are you travelling to?'
'Ireland,' said Timothy, his reply brought a pleasant smile.
She was twenty-two or three, with a neat hairstyle, and a good figure. He wondered should he try to get to know her better. When she arrived with his beer he noticed a ring on her finger and he was disappointed.
He'd sit and enjoy his drink for a while, eventually going for a stroll around Liverpool where the boats were bare of all sail. The wind howled like a starved wolf, so he stayed away from the quay edge in case he'd get blown into the sea or soaked by an incoming wave. He turned to walk towards the city when he noticed a lady standing in a doorway.
'Hello,' he heard her say. He looked and smiled.
She nodded back, smiled and winked as if to invite him to come closer, being a lady of the night. He laughed knowing he didn't want to move in those circles.
This incident took his mind back to a girl he knew at school. Thinking about her engaged his mind in deep fantasy. He was well up near the city centre when he recovered. The weather was not as bad here as down at

the docks. He ventured into another tavern where there were a lot of people. He suspected they were seamen as they all wore the same caps made from neat knitted wool with a turn up across the forehead. The smell of smoke mixed with ale made him breath deeply. He could see between the tables and stools there was a space for dancing.

'Come on lovey let's dance,' one of the ladies said to him, holding her arms up and waltzing him as he made his way to the counter for a drink. She could see he was young and shy. She'd flirt a little with him because of his youth and inexperience. Laughing he held her and danced closer to the bar.

'Thank you very much,' he shouted. She gave him a kiss on the cheek and everyone started laughing.

As he got his drink, he thought that these sailors were really enjoying the weather, singing and dancing and having a right good time. All the men lifted their glasses to him, when he turned to face them.

'Hello! Sir,' their greetings and broad smiles made Timothy feel relaxed.

The music from the violin got louder and a few of the fellows grabbed the girls and started dancing. Timothy watched, laughed and sang along with them and was accepted as if he was one of them. In his amazement at the antics of the women and the sailors, he didn't notice that there was a bit of tension.

'What the hell are you trying to do?' shouted one of the sailors as he drew out and hit a man a blow in the face. This caused the girl he was dancing with to almost split her head on the bar.

'You stupid old fool,' shouted the sailor, swinging to hit him back.

'Don't you hit my mate,' said another man busting him in the face.

The men waded into each other with some trying to stop the row, while others were so drunk they didn't know what they were doing. Some men were upset that their girls were dancing with the wrong fellows. Jealousy "being the great starter of rows" sure got this one going. Timothy noticed a man falling down, as a mug swirled through the air, hopping off another man's ear. Timothy's table was turned over, spilling his drink on top of him when he was pushed to the ground. The weight of the man lying across him and the blow he received against the table almost knocked him out. As he was getting up, someone grabbed him and muttered. 'Give me a hand will you? If I don't get out of here I'll be killed.'

'The way things are going here I think we're both going to die,' said Timothy, as he lifted him up off the floor.

Hearing women screaming and men cursing and swearing, Timothy dragged this man along. He felt the scrape of the doors as he and his mate were helped forcibly through to the street. The wet and the cold sobered the situation quickly. The fellow he pulled from the bar didn't seem to be aware of what had happened, or realise he was out in the street with blood streaming from his ear and his head. Timothy kept going, while his companion just hung on to him. He looked back and saw the bar door with people all around, no doubt with sore heads, arms, eyes and noses. He considered himself lucky to have escaped alive. At least he was more alive than this fellow he was helping.

'Where exactly are you going,' Timothy asked him. 'Do you think you're badly hurt? I see blood coming from around your ear. Stop and I'll have a better look.'

He could see a deep gash, which needed attention. The man seemed to suffer more from drink than his wounds. Timothy walking along could feel the soreness in his leg, elbow and arm, and the strong smell of drink from his clothes.

'Where are we going to get you home,' said Timothy again.

'On to the docks. Would you mind if I lean on your shoulder?' he slurred, as he stumbled and almost fell.

'It's not far, just straight down and turn right at the bottom of the street.'

'I sail with a ship,' he belched. 'It's docked there for the last three days, and if the weather is not as bad as it was, I think we'll be sailing soon. Next time we meet I'll buy you a drink. It was good there tonight until some goat started the row. You must admit there were some good-looking women there. A fellow might have made a bit of progress with one of them had it not been for the idiot.'

When they arrived at the ship Timothy had to help his drunken mate up the gangplank and down to his cabin where he handed him to another sailor.

'What happened? He was asked.

'There was a row in the tavern and we were lucky to get away uninjured.'

'No doubt it was over some woman,' said the sailor, 'would you like a drink?'

'No thanks, I think we've seen enough of the drink tonight.'

Timothy was glad to be going back to his boarding house, as he knew he'd be sailing tomorrow. He was thinking of what the life of a sailor was like. They had a reputation for drinking and wild women. It was a lonely life, weeks at sea and it could be dangerous. He wondered what was the attraction and supposed it was the seeing of new places.

Chapter 3

The months passed quickly as did the trouble with the police. Settled life continued at its normal pace. In order to make a living the O'Shea family got back into the rhythm of life's survival.
'Come on you two,' their father called to Mary and Peter. 'We'll head off to Spring Lake and do a bit of fishing and maybe catch a rabbit or two.'
They quickly gathered their fishing poles and a few snares. Mary could see the shine of the lake from the hill as she walked along. She felt happy, the warm gentle breeze was blowing her hair, and she could feel its caress on her face. The bright clouds against the blue sky looked like mountains, and she wondered what it would be like to climb one of them.
'Mary pay attention to me for a minute.' She looked at her father. 'This is the spot on the ground where you set a snare, he pointed with his finger, just between where the rabbit hops and lands. That way the wire will catch around its neck and choke it.'
'That's cruel isn't it?'
'Yes it is, but it's the only kind of dinner we'll get if we get a dinner at all. So make sure you learn all about catching them.'
After a while Peter arrived back to the lakeside with two rabbits, delighted with himself.
'Listen a minute you two, you have to take care when you are skinning a rabbit. Look after the fur, it can be used in the making of clothes.'
They stood and watched him skin the little animal at the side of the lake.
'Peter, look and check to see if the fur is damaged in any way. When we get home you can stretch the skins and leave them hanging in the shed until they are dry.'

Mary saw a creativeness in her father when he made scarves from the skins.

'Do you know something Mary, the landlords won't allow anyone onto their land to catch rabbits and it's not even their land,' Peter sounded annoyed.

Mary went back to her fishing, watching the float carefully to see would it dip in the water. She saw the glimmer of the sun on the lake, a waterhen with her chicks, way over on the far side, and that little movement in the weeds looked like an otter. She liked being here by the lakeside where there were a lot of birds and small animals, she could sit relax and dream.

'Quick! Quick!' they heard her shout.

'Pull on that line Mary, then ease it off gently, let the fish think he's getting away,' her father helped her. 'Now ease it back in towards the shore.'

She could see that he was more excited about the fishing then she was.

'A-ha look at what I caught,' she shouted, laughing and feeling great as she pulled a fish from the water. It was a big pike it would make a nice dinner.

'Look there at that bush Mary, it's time to pick the blackberries again. Don't the seasons go round quickly?'

'I'll go and see my friend about picking them next week.'

Mary and Ann attended school together. Mrs. Smith was their teacher. Being a neighbour and a friend of the family she made sure that the local children got a good education. Between her schooling and the extra education Mary got from her mother, she was a well educated, young lady. She had a talent for art, and sketching.

A few days later she headed off to see if Ann would go picking blackberries with her.

Walking along she always had her dog 'Captain' by her side. He was friendly and had a tail that curved up to touch the centre of his back with a shiny black coat of hair. He dashed in and out of the river that ran along the road as dogs always do. Mary got a surprise when the Dooley brothers jumped out of the hedge. The young fellow was laughing, while the older lad came up to her.

'What the hell are you doing here you snivelling little witch?'

'It's none of your business,' she said.

'I'll show you whose business it is,' as he grabbed her and started to horse around.

Mary knew Patrick Dooley. He was a bit of a bully but she felt she could look after herself. He put his hands on her pretending to push her, but he was really trying to feel her.

'Stop that you cheeky brat', she shouted.

'You should not be here, this is not your territory. I'm in charge here,' he replied smartly.

Mary could see this fellow was going to try to have his way, she became anxious. He was stronger than she was, so the more she told him to stop the bolder he got, he tried to kiss her.

'How dare you try to kiss me,' she shouted loudly, giving him a hard slap on the cheek and scraping him with her nail.

'Take that you pup and leave me alone,' she said in a crying voice.

His younger brother did not realise what was going on, and thought it was funny.

Mary was getting afraid. 'Get away from me you bully,' she cried, trying to hit him again.

The more she tried to stop him the more he pushed himself against her.

'If you don't leave me alone, I'll tell my brothers on you and they'll fix you. She could see her threat was wasted, because he was excited.

She felt his hands on her, she got nervous and tears began to fall, as she shouted at him.

'Stop it, please, please stop it. She slipped and fell on her knee and he saw her leg and became more excited.
She saw her dog Captain, was lying on the ground with his paws out in front of him, snarling and shaking his head. He bared his teeth and gave a low growl.
'Captain, Captain,' she shouted, and pointed her hand at her attacker. The dog sprang into action like a lion.
Mary's tensions left her she was amazed at the power of her dog. She pointed at her attacker and said, 'Hiss''Hiss.' The dog leapt to bite him and he backed off quickly. Seeing that the dog was in control she moved closer and again went "Hiss" "Hiss." The dog quickly had the two boys standing in the river. The young lad was crying, she felt sorry for him, so she went and held his hand. 'Don't cry, it will be all right, that brother of yours caused all this trouble.'
She turned to the older lad with tears in her eyes and pointing her finger at him said. 'I'm going to tell my brothers about you. They'll sort you out you stupid brat.'
Patrick turned to her in a pleading voice and said. 'Please don't Mary, I'm sorry, please, don't tell them.'
As she wiped away her tears and tried to control herself, she noticed that all his excitement was gone.
'I'll think about it. Now take your brother home and tell him you're sorry for causing the trouble.'
She called his young brother over, he was afraid. She held him by the shoulders and gave him a hug saying: 'It will be all right, you're a good boy, stop crying.'
Mary gave the dog a couple of hugs and left the boys standing in the wet. She wondered how things would have gone, and what would have happened had she not had Captain with he. Her ordeal with the brat, while frightening, made her think about herself. Why was he trying to put his hands on me... was he attracted to me? When she threatened to tell her brothers, he was apologetic and did feel sorry and afraid. She decided not to tell anyone yet, as she knew he was not a bad

lad. Thinking of his younger brother and feeling sorry for him she made her way home.

'Hello Mary,' her sister Cathleen greeted her. 'Did you see your friend Ann?'

'No, I met the Dooley boys. We talked then I came on home.'

She didn't bother to tell Cathleen about her ordeal.

A few days later Mary called on her friend Ann and they went picking blackberries. The weather was beautiful they could feel the heat of the sun.

'Look across the field Ann, do you see those three horsemen. They're the police and they're heading towards that house. They're probably going to collect rent from those people and if they haven't got it they'll be thrown out and their farm taken from them. Isn't it terrible?'

'We'll hide in here Mary and watch until they go away.'

The police went inside the house and came back out quickly dragging a man with them. They were beating and kicking him and he fell on the ground. The girls could see him holding himself with the pain.

'This is illegal you are not supposed to be making this stuff you know. They kicked him a few times.

'We'll make sure you never make it again,' said one of them, laughing as he lit the thatched roof of the house.

Mary had seen two men leaving just before the peelers arrived. The police had discovered a poteen still and burned it down. The men who had left must have seen the smoke, so they arrived back to help their friend. When Mary got home that evening, her father greeted her at the door.

'You girls did well today,' he said pointing towards her two cans of blackberries. 'Did Ann pick as much as you?

'Yes she picked about the same.'

'We saw the police burn the old house where we were picking the berries father.'

'Yes but what you didn't know was that Tom and I were inside with Gerry McColl making poteen? We were lucky we went off to get some grain, when that mob came and gave Gerry a hiding. Those men are a shower of thugs, they please themselves just because they work for the British.'

'I agree with you father, the way they treated that poor man was terrible.'

'It's happening all the time Mary, so don't let it annoy you.' Come on we'll have our tea and forget all about them. Mary could feel that her Father was beginning to accept that this was the way life was going to be. She looked at his lined face most of his red hair was gone. His attitude was thoughtful. He spoke with a soft gentle voice, and she could see that age and times of trouble, had their effect on him.

On her way home from Ann's house one evening Mary met her sister struggling with a can of water. She helped her to carry it.

'Uncle Sean is inside talking to our mother and father. He has news for you Mary and I think it's good.'

'Come on then, tell me what is it?'

'Oh no, you go on in and find out for yourself.'

Mary went inside and was greeted by her uncle. 'Hello, how are you Mary? My but you have grown since I saw you last'.

Chapter 4

Timothy entered his lodgings and went straight up to the bar to get a drink. He sat down and allowed the tensions of the night to drain from him. He saw the girl who wore the ring behind the bar. At least she was pretty to look at, as the horrible thoughts of the night tramped through his mind. In a year or so school will finish he thought. He wondered should he stay here in England and find work, or should he go back home to Ireland. He liked Ireland and he got on well with the people. His parents were English, he was born in Ireland, but because he went to school in England he had an English accent. Everything was getting mixed up he thought.

When he bought his ticket to travel the next day, one of the fellows remarked to him. 'You'll test your sailing ability tonight,' he was laughing.

Timothy went back to his lodgings, got his gear and headed for the ship. When he went on board, he realised it was the same boat he'd brought the drunken sailor to, last evening. He threw his bag below and came up on to the deck and watched the sailors getting ready to sail.

There was something nice about sailing ships. Maybe it was the way they quietly slipped through the water, silent and sure. He looked at the way the sails filled with air and this caused the ship to gather speed. The way the sailors knew exactly when to hoist the sail, and safely navigate out of port. After a while the sway, the gentle motion and the chilly air, had him thinking of his bed.

A tap on the back made him turn to look at a man with a bandaged head and his arm covered up to his elbow.

'I thought it was you. I've just come up from my cabin now. What do you think of all these bandages, don't I look great?' said his injured friend.

'Well, at least you look sore,' said Timothy laughing. 'You were lucky you know. How's the head?'

'Ah sure I'll survive. So you're going to Ireland?'

'Yeah, that's where I'm from. I'm only over here at College.'

'We stop in Ireland every time we come over from America. By the way, my name is John Ellickson and my father William is the captain. I was lucky you gave me a hand last night. It was getting to be a great night until the trouble started.'

'Yes I was just beginning to enjoy myself.

'Ireland is a troubled part of the world Timothy. We have taken a lot of people to America over the last number of years.'

'I'm studying to be an engineer I might go to America when I qualify.'

'There will be plenty of use for your type of work over there as things are only getting started. There are thousands of people arriving every day from all over the world. I heard that out west the government is giving land away for next to nothing, they're only trying to get people to take it. They say that the west is as big as the ocean we cross to get there.'

'How long does it take for you to sail over?' said Timothy.

'If we sail to New Orleans, it could take six maybe seven weeks, New York five or six weeks -- a lot depends on the weather. A young man like you would like it out there, but it's a tough place I heard.'

Timothy noticed that sometimes when John laughed, he winced.

'That cut on the head is causing you a bit of pain.'

'Yeah, it does sometimes.'

'Timothy! I'm going to lie down for an hour, then we won't be far from docking and we'll have a drink before you leave.'
Timothy nodded and watched his soreheaded friend, go to his cabin.

As he looked into the water, he began to think about what he was going to do when he finished school. Looking in the distance he saw land. The thought of America appealed to him. It brought thoughts of a fresh start and anything he would do, or had, would be achieved for himself, by him. Leaning over the rail of the ship he watched the bow cut through the water like a big knife. Overhead he could see the seagulls glide as though floating on nothing. He wondered exactly what did hold them up. Looking up he acknowledged a call from his heavily bandaged friend. As he entered the cabin, he was greeted with a handshake.
'You are?'
'Timothy Melen.'
'So you are the young man who helped my son to his cabin the other night. For that I must say thanks. 'Here take this mug?' It was half full of whiskey.
'As you probably know my name is William Ellickson. If you are ever in any kind of trouble, or have a problem that I can help you with, either here in Ireland, England or even America, just give me a shout. You will always be able to contact me through the shipping office. Who knows, perhaps sometime in the future you might want to take a trip with us, I must say thank you again.' he shook Timothy's hand saying: 'You will have to allow me to go. We're not far from docking.'

Timothy finished his drink and felt a bit giddy getting off the ship. He noticed that nearly all the sails were down as they sailed up the river. Walking away from the boat he looked back and gave a wave to the two men. He headed for the coach and home.

As the coach rolled along he saw the cattle in the fields, all the houses were small and whitewashed.

The Bluebell's Mystery

Sometimes he saw a man or a woman out digging, probably potatoes. He slept, to wake almost at his stop. From there he walked and enjoyed the countryside, soon he arrived home.

Chapter 5

'Ah, there you are Mary,' said her father. 'Your Uncle Sean has some good news for you.' Mary looked at her Uncle and could see that he looked a lot like her father. A little bit older, he was broad shouldered and slightly stooped by age.

'As you know Mary, I work at the Melen's Estate and I was talking to Mrs.Ward. She's in charge of the kitchen staff. She said there's a job available for a girl of your age. Would you be interested in working there?'
'Yes I would and you can tell her that I will be delighted to take the job.'

Later that evening Peter and Tom arrived home and over tea they discussed with their Uncle Sean how things were going at the Melen's estate. When Peter heard that Mary was going to work for an English landlord he got upset.
'You should not go to work there Mary, they're a rotten shower of British dogs. Don't you realise that these are the very people who have this country in the state it's in? You should understand that a few years ago when this country was in the grip of famine, these people didn't lift a hand to help us. If anything, they used it to help themselves to more of our land by allowing us to die of starvation.'

In her shock at his abusive attitude towards her, Mary shouted back.
'It's none of your business Peter, I'm getting a chance of a job and I want to use it to make a few pounds and then I'll be able to do what I want. If I don't go to work there, I'll still be standing here in a year's time and what good will that do anybody? So don't be so aware of what I'm doing and be more concerned about yourself. You never had a job and if you don't make

things change you never will. You have stayed at home working on our farm since you turned sixteen, isn't that right?' She screamed at him.

'You silly bitch, don't you realise that if I could get the money I'd go to America as quick as that,' holding up his hand and clicking his fingers. 'Do you think I want to stay at home. The British are here and they have taken everything from us and they want more. If we try to fight back we are either put in jail, or sent to Australia on one of their death ships.

This outburst took a lot of his energy and he was almost crying. Mary could see this and it tugged at her heart.

'Right then, I'll tell you what, you say nothing to me for going to work for these dogs as you like to call them. If I make a few pounds I'll lend you the money to go to America, and when you get there you can send for me. Who knows, we might both end up over there yet.'

She didn't understand how hard it was for a man to get any kind of work at that time in Ireland. She didn't know that all the young men and women were trying to get to the new world as they called it. The arguing and the fighting upset everyone in the house.

Jumping from her chair Cathleen shouted. 'Don't do that.' She threw her arms around Peter to stop him from hitting Mary.

'Listen here a minute you two, my boyfriend Jim was told about a man who was helping people to go to America. He had been over there and he discovered that land was being sold cheaply by the State. Due to the terrible situation of things in Ireland he came back and decided to take people out there and arrange to get them a piece of land. If we had money we could look into this, what do you lot think of that?' Cathleen shouted.

'Okay then if it's possible to make that happen, let's do it,' said Peter. 'Hopefully what you say is true.'

The Bluebell's Mystery

Cathleen felt great. She was the one who took the bitterness out of the argument.

'Ask Jim to find out more about this particular man and America.'

Mary knew that the job was an opportunity to try and change her situation. She understood Peter's concern for her but she had to go.

   With all the arguing and fighting, Mary or Peter didn't notice that their mother was outside the window. She could hear the row this kind of thing upset her very much. She felt bad for Peter and could understand his feelings. She didn't like it, that Mary was going to work for an English landlord but she'd earn a wage, sure that's all that matters at this time. Surely Peter can understand that? She hoped that things would work out for Mary.

Rose remembered back to when she got married. Everyone in the country was suffering from terrible need, then the potato crop failed. Friends and neighbours of hers were dying of hunger and there was no need for it. She thought of how her family all suffered at the hands of the established order of the time. The landlord on three occasions was going to throw them off their small farm. He had taken most of their land as payment for rent owed. Her brothers spent their youth stealing and trying to make a living, they got their chance and went to America. It was the start of the famine they were lucky. After a few years the effects of the starvation and hunger took it's toll on her parents health. When they passed away she felt alone. This loss of her brothers and her parents broke her heart. Years later she heard from America that they were all right and things had worked well for them.

Hearing this row between Peter and Mary and the mention of America made her wonder was it all going to happen again.

The Bluebell's Mystery

What she heard Cathleen say about the man from America was the best piece of news she had heard in a long time. It's no harm to let Mary go to work for the Melen's she thought. Anything that helped her family to get out of this situation would be a blessing. She thanked God, even if it did mean her children were emigrating. She recalled the bad times, but not all the British were bad. Some of the landlords, seeing how terrible the situation was, did go out of their way to help the Irish. It meant a great deal to some, but sadly, not enough of the landlords had their counterpart's compassion.

Rose, in her tears, considered herself one of the lucky ones. She moved a little further away from the house to a spot in the garden where everything had gone wild. She felt guilty for not looking after her roses. She loved the wildness of her garden, the different greens. The dark, the bright, and the green of the palm tree. In her memory she could see her roses, beautiful red, she had their imprint on her mind day and night, summer or winter.

She noticed something dash into the hedge, no doubt a rabbit. Rose thought about what James had said to Mary, to use the situation for our benefit.

Chapter 6

His father greeted him with a handshake and a smile. 'Hello! Timothy, how was the crossing, was it rough? I had to stay one night in Liverpool because of the gales.' 'The weather was bad here, I didn't think you'd come at all... at least you got here safely that's what counts.'Thaddaeus was Timothy's father's proper name, but people called him Ted. With a name like that he could not blame them. He was born in Ireland and his father had been an officer in the British army, as indeed had his father before him. He thought the Irish were an awkward lot. They'd talk to him, laugh and joke and then turn to each other and start speaking in a different language. He always suspected they were talking about him. This suspicion made him a little anti -Irish. Due to this the people who were working on the estate considered him, cranky and contrary.

He recalled the Famine years and how people were starving. One day he went to the village looking for someone to come and harvest his grain. He called to a house and when the door was answered he got a shock. 'Hello,' he said. The woman who asked him inside looked like a skeleton, he could see that she was starving.

When he saw the condition of the family in the house he was badly shocked, so he took her husband back to his estate showed him what his job would be, and asked. 'Is there a possibility you could get a few more men to help with the harvesting.'

'Yes Indeed I will,' said 'Patrick.

'You can start that job tomorrow, now go out to the field and take whatever food you need to feed your family.'

'Thank you very much Ted.'

It's said that after seeing the condition that the people were in Ted tried to help them. The fact that he was the landlord did not necessarily mean he owned the land, as he in turn had to make payments to his peers in England. He tried to balance his expenses to the land Lords, and be as humane as possible to the Irish people, but he was in a no-win situation.

It's said that he paid a lot of the expenses to get people to America. Perhaps that was to favour his position. Things in Ireland were changing for the better Politically, but the famine years had taken their toll on Ted's health. He relied mostly on his son Fred to run the estate.

Timothy was delighted to be home. He was enjoying his holiday. He felt good getting a break from his studying. He and Fred were on their way to the fields at the back of the lake to check the cattle and harvest the potatoes. After the terrible years of the famine potatoes were still the main food of the people, although the farming community had switched to other types of vegetable growing and grain.

'Timothy, when is your schooling finished?'

'In approximately a year and three months.'

'Do you think you will come back here to work on the farm?'

'I don't think I'll bother with farming. I'll stay with the engineering, I find it interesting.'

'Maybe it's just as well you're thinking that way,' 'I think that both of us running this farm would cause problems.'

Anyway you'll always have your engineering to fall back on.' Timothy was amazed at the attitude of his brother.

'I'll probably stay on in England, Timothy's voice faded as they heard the cry, help-help. They looked and started running in the direction of the lake.

'Come on,' Fred gestured with his hand, 'look at that lad splashing in the water.'

Fred grabbed a branch and pushed it out towards the young lad, hitting him on the head. Grabbing at anything the boy clutched the branch and felt himself being pulled towards the shore. Timothy up to his waist in water put his hand out and helped pull the boy out of the water. The young lad was crying and shivering with the cold.

'What the hell had you out there so deep. You nearly drowned you brat. You frightened the living daylights out of us. Fred sounded emotional and shocked. 'Do you realise if we hadn't been around you'd probably be drowned by now?'

The young fellow in his short trousers, knee length socks and old boots was unable to stop shivering from the cold of the icy water. Bursting out crying he said. 'I was out at the end of the fallen tree fishing and I slipped and fell in.'

'Do you realise you're trespassing and you shouldn't be here at all.'

With the water running down into his boots and shaking with every breath he took, the little boy replied.

'I know I'm sorry I was trying to catch a fish.'

'Did you have any luck?'

'Yes there's two small ones over there.'

'What's your name anyway and where do you live?'

'Martin McCabe, I live over at Rockchapel.'

'Well get your fish and get to hell out of here and don't you ever come back, do you hear that you brat? If I ever catch you fishing off that tree again I'll have you arrested.'

'Hold on a minute Fred, this lad almost drowned, can't you see he's in a bad way? Look he's shivering. There's no need for you to attack him.'

'I'm trying to frighten him, because we must make sure he doesn't come back here again. If he wants to fish then let him stand on the shore. Who cares about the

brat? What difference will it make to you or me if he gets pneumonia.'
'You go and get changed Fred, then go over and check on the cattle and see about the potatoes. I'll follow along after you.'
'What are you, going to do Timothy?'
'I'm taking this brat around to Mrs.Ward. Let the women look after him.' 'He's in a terrible state, look at him. Get your fishing rod and your fish young man and come along with me.'
'Please don't tell the Melens on me,' said Martin.
'Okay we won't, but make sure you don't go out on that tree again, it's too dangerous.'
'Hello Timothy who's that young lad with you,' said Mrs. Ward. 'He's soaking wet what happened him?'
'His name is Martin McCabe, and he slipped and fell into the lake. He's cold and wet. Will you look after him?'

The boy was taken inside to the kitchen by the ladies. Some of them knew who he was his clothes were changed and put in a bag with his fish. He was given something to eat and sent home.

As he walked home the fact that he had almost drowned was something he would always remember. The way the ladies fussed over him he'd never forget. He didn't realise that they were happy, things worked out for one so young.
'Well Fred, how are things here. Are these fellows doing their work okay?'
'They got some work done but they could have done a lot more the lazy lot. I'll have to stand over them and watch every move they make.'
'I got that young lad away alright,' said Timothy.
'We should have sent him home the way he was.'
'There's no need for that attitude Fred, leave him alone. He didn't do anything wrong.'
They picked and pitted the potatoes for the next few weeks and it was hard work.

The weeks slipped by and winter had lost its grip. Timothy could see the change in the seasons by the new growth on the shrubs and trees. The sycamore was the one he liked best. It showed its awakening by the new shoots and its fresh deep green colour. Soon he'd have to go back to school. He felt happy he'd been party to saving a life. Reluctantly he walked towards the horse and trap that took him as far as the coach road and back to England.

Chapter 7

Mary had the thoughts of her row with Peter on her mind as she walked the country road on her way to work. She had to travel a mile-and-a-half to the village and another mile to Melen's Demesne. Although she felt anxious and excited, she was aware of her surroundings. Winter was beginning to lose its grip; the green was starting to fill the trees. This was nature at its best, with wildlife all a buzz; she was happy walking along this morning.
She was unaware how attractive she looked. Her long reddish hair hung loosely down around her shoulders, and she kept her hat pulled down tightly against the cold breeze that chilled her face. Even on such a cold morning her slender figure would make people's heads turn. A fox chasing a rabbit almost knocked her over. Mary realised that due to her he'd missed his breakfast. Its bright coat inspired her... the red colour of its fur, the thought of putting those shades into clothes, coats and dresses. The colours of the fox and the pheasant filled her mind with thoughts of beautiful shapes. She thought about the dress she was wearing, and all the work and effort she and her sister had put into it. The dress was oddly shaped because she had experimented with new and crazy designs.
　She remembered walking up and down the house modelling it, her sister and mother laughing. They made smart comments, and the more they laughed, the more she'd put on the fancy walk. Cathleen got her turn, and if the boys were there it became a party.
'What do you think of this dress Cathleen?'
'It's nice, but it's not normal.'
'Should I wear it to my first job?'
'Yes indeed,' said Cathleen laughing. 'It will open an eye or two.'

As a joke, she said. 'Why don't you try and get into the business of making dresses.'
She didn't realise this idea had haunted Mary's mind since she was a young girl.

Today was market day; the farmers passed her with their horses and carts, and some had cattle. The better off farmers would have a mare or a stallion for sale. These horses had their tails and their manes plaited, and they were groomed to perfection, their hair looked better then most of the ladies.
Her dreaming was interrupted when she met a friend from school, Peg Gartlan who was standing at her gate.
'Hello Mary, you know we were only talking about you last week.'
"Ah," so you were talking about me? I hope you were saying nice things.' Mary started to laugh. 'May I ask what were they saying and who was doing the talking?'
'Do you remember a fellow called Andy McEntee, he went to school with you. He lives somewhere out on the Blaney road. Remember we used to laugh at the McEntee, McNamee names the way they rhymed? He asked me to find out if you would go out with him. Now the question is Mary, are you going to go out with him, or are you going to break his heart?'
In a low serious tone Mary said. 'Do you think it would it break his heart, if I don't go out with him?' They started laughing. Peg continued on. 'He seems a nice fellow; he has changed since you seen him last.'
'What do you think Peg, should I meet him?'
'To tell you the truth Mary, if I wasn't going with Jim O'Brian I'd go with him myself, he's a handsome looking fellow.'
'Seeing as you put it that way, I'll go out with him.'
'Anyway Mary, where are you going at this time of the morning?'
'Would you believe I got a job in Melen's Demesne.'
'That's great Mary. It's hard to get a job nowadays, but you'd want to watch yourself there.'

'Why do you say that Peg?'
'I knew a girl who worked in one of those estates. She got involved with an English man and she was told she'd be better off out of the country.'
'Don't worry about me I'm not going to get involved with those people.'
Peg's brother Tom stepped from the house.
'Hello Mary, are you coming my way?'
'Yes, if you are going through the village.'
'Let's walk then.'
Peg waved goodbye to them.
Further on up the village she saw her father and her brother Tom, she knew Peter was around somewhere. They had a few animals with them that they must have taken in for John Curtis.
Mary wondered what kind of a place America was. She imagined herself going, perhaps meeting her husband there. If Peter went he might take her with him. Right now she had to go and find her own way, it would give her independence. She felt bad about her row with Peter and knew how difficult she could be. I'll give him the fare to America and use the British for the benefit of my family. She was hoping Peter was not mixed up in anything that was anti-British.
Mary's father was surprised to see her.
'I thought you would have been gone to work by now.'
"Ah, but I don't have to be in until ten."
'You know you are going to have to keep going or you'll be late.'
"All right, I'll see you later.' She looked at Tom he winked and smiled. She nodded and went on.
Both her father and Tom were glad to see her leave. They knew the police would be poking around. Mary didn't know anything and it was as well to keep it that way.
Three policemen arrived to check on the animals. How in heaven's name they were going to find an animal that had been stolen was beyond Tom and his father,

seeing as there was no branding or marking of any kind. One of them was the sergeant who had him hammered at the Curtis farm.

'Ah, Hello! Tom, you do remember the time we met before,' he said laughing.

'I do indeed, how could I forget.'

'Well I'm asking the same questions, exactly how many cattle have you got with you today?'

'Well I'm giving you exactly the same answers, drag your arse over there and ask the cattle themselves. They'll have no trouble talking to an idiot like you, isn't that right?' Tom started to laugh.

'You don't talk to me like that, or I'll get my men to give you another hammering.'

'You had better get a few extra lads.'

At this stage there were about four farmers over to talk to Tom.

'You go to hell but remember we'll meet again.'

A little while later, the sergeant arrived back alone and said to Tom.

'Let's talk sense Tom and let's be more civil with each other. How many animals have you got there?'

'Five,' Tom replied; 'some of them belong to John Curtis.'

Tom wondered about this sergeant fellow. He fitted the bill as being pro-British, yet some of the things he said seemed more of a warning than a threat. Even John Curtis wondered about him.

'Have you sold any cattle yet?'

'No, things are slow today.'

'Well I advise you to stop stealing as you may have an informer in your midst,' he smiled. 'I know exactly what's going on, the animals are stolen and switched to different farms.'

Tom wondered was Farrell trying to infiltrate this movement or did he really know all about it? Perhaps he was a part of it, and working for the British at the same time?

'That's not a bad idea you know,' remarked Tom. 'If I ever decide to get into the cattle stealing business I might use your idea. Do you think I should put it past your police friends first?'
'I don't think that would be smart. It would be better for someone like you, to have someone like me on your side while I'm in the police, don't you think?'
Sergeant Farrell gave a wry smile, and left Tom wondering.
There were quite a few big English landlord estates around this area. In between the big farms there were a good lot of smallholdings. These farmers had a system whereby cattle were taken and sent to different farms that bordered each other. When the police arrived to accuse the farmer they found themselves embroiled in a row about who, the land belonged to.

Mary thought how lucky she was to get the job. Her uncle told her that if she did not take it someone else would. In her dreaming and wondering about the boys, she didn't realise she was at her place of work. She pulled her mind together just before knocking on the door, feeling anxious. She noticed it wasn't just a big house, it was more of a castle. The main entrance had a beautiful ornamental gate, with castellated walls to the side. There were four big towers that made the house square, with a long area going out from the back. Yes, it was a castle. She paused, knocked, then waited a minute or so. Looking across the lawns she noticed a trap with two people in it coming from the back of the house, heading towards the main gate. The voice she heard came from behind her. When she looked round a girl dressed in an apron and a short coat said: 'Hello, I'm Teresa Boyle, you must be Mary O'Shea.'
'That's right.'
'Welcome to Melen's Demesne,' she smiled shaking Mary's hand.
'We have been expecting you, so come on and I'll introduce you to the rest of the ladies.'

Teresa brought her down the steps to the kitchen. Mary could feel the heat of the cooker, thinking how nice it must be working here in the winter.
'Come over here Mary and I'll introduce you to Mrs. Ward.'
Shaking her hand, Mary could see she had brown hair tucked neatly under her white hat. She was standing close to the cast iron cooker tending to the pots and pans, with breakfast and dinner in the process of being made. At the end of the table Mary saw cabbage, turnips and carrots waiting to be prepared for cooking.
'Hello Mary, I spoke to your uncle Sean, and you look just as he described you. Teresa, take Mary and bring her on a quick tour of the house and then you can both start and get these vegetables ready.' She pointed towards the table. Mary was introduced to the rest of the staff, most of whom were older than she was. Teresa looked about the same age as Mary. Her black hair was tied back neatly and the dress she wore with the white apron made her look attractive.
'Mary you and I will be sleeping in the same room.'
'Well at least I'll have company.'
'I was told that this castle was built about three hundred years ago, the grounds total about four hundred acres, and it needs about twenty people to keep the place going.'
'What kind of a place is this to work in?' asked Mary.
'I'm only here three weeks myself and the only people I've met are Mrs. Melen and the kitchen staff. The work can be demanding at times. However, most of the staff are pleasant and easy to work with. Some of them can be a bit contrary at times but you'll soon get to know them.'

    Stepping into the drawing room Mary saw a suit of armour standing against the wall, it looked like a real man.
'Isn't he a handsome man with all his battle equipment. Wars must have been terribly rough way back then.'

She felt bad having to walk on the rug that was on the floor with its fancy designs.

'Yes, they must have been mighty men back in those days,' said Teresa laughing.

On the wall behind them were two old-type musket guns.

'Imagine getting a blow from a sword like that, there was no chance of survival.'

'Wait until you see the ballroom Mary, it must be great when there's a ball here.'

'Isn't it huge? Look at the floor and the stage, there are candelabras and mirrors everywhere.'

'Imagine being here at a party.'

'It's no harm to dream about things like that Teresa anyway it's most unlikely it will ever happen to people like you and I.'

Teresa took a few steps across the floor as if to dance. Turning the corner they met Mrs. Melen, Teresa introduced Mary to her.

'Mrs. Ward told me to show Mary around the house. She's starting work here this morning.'

'I'm pleased to meet you Mary. I hope you'll be happy working here. I must hurry now, but no doubt we'll talk again,' she smiled.

'She's quite a pleasant woman Teresa isn't she?'

'Yes, we get on well with her. Her husband and their son Fred are not as nice as she is. They have another son Timothy. He's at college in England but I never met him'

Mary soon fell into the rhythm of things in her new job, a seven o'clock rise in the mornings to prepare the breakfast. She and Teresa became good friends and they made their own clothes. They worked together and dressed each other in the most unusual styles, as it was something they both enjoyed. However, early mornings and dressmaking at night would see them very tired.

'Do you know Mary that I go to the ceili sometimes? Would you like to come along?'

'Oh, yes I'd be delighted to go.'

The following Friday night they went to the village for a night's ceiling and Mary met her friend Peg Gartlan.

'Ah, so we meet again! I have news for you, your friend is here tonight, so come on I'll introduce you to him.'

Peg was right. This Andy McEntee fellow is quite handsome. They danced together, and she enjoyed his company because he was nice and friendly.

After a few reels with him Mary went back to her friends.

One of the girls jokingly remarked. 'Where did you girls get the dresses you're wearing? I suppose you borrowed them from some of the grand ladies in Melens.'

'No we did not,' said Mary. 'We made them ourselves. What do you think of them anyway?' She twirled round to show off the skirt.

'I must say you went a bit overboard but they are nice.'

'Would you wear one of these dresses Evelyn?'

'Yes of course I would, you can lend me that one next week,' she started laughing.

Mary had a good night with Andy, he was alright kissing but a bit over-anxious with his hands.

'Can I see you again Mary?'

'I'll probably see you at the next ceili,' she said, keeping him wondering.

Chapter 8
Matthew 1960

These were the youthful years of enjoyment for Matthew O'Neill. He was thirteen years of age, and he and his friends spent their time swimming in Creevy Lake robbing orchards and herding cattle like the cowboys. They were told to stop because they were running the fat off them. He was the youngest of a family of seven, they lived in a cottage roughly a mile from the town of Carrick.

After spending nine years at the Christian Brothers school at the top of the town he was now attending the Technical College. This was a mixed school where boys and girls attended. Matthew liked this. He was good at woodwork and metalwork and he excelled at history, this was his favourite subject.

'Listen boys,' said Mr. Kearns, 'you'll be getting your holidays soon and I've got an exercise I'd like you to do during that time.'

'I hope it's interesting,' said Terry Daly. 'We're supposed to be on our holidays you know.'

'This is a simple exercise but it will keep you occupied, and some of you will find it worthwhile and interesting. If you like, you can look back on your family tree, you'll be amazed at what you'll find out about your ancestors. For instance, how many of you have relations who went to America during the Famine years?'

In answer to this question half of the class put their hands up.

'Sir,' Matthew called for the teacher's attention.

'What is it?'

'My mother told me that her two brothers went to America in the year 1913, and she never saw them again. She was only a young girl at that time.'

'Thanks for that information Matthew. You see class there's an interesting story already. Again I must stress to you to talk to your parents, as they will relate to you some happy stories about your ancestors, and some very sad ones. Have a look in the local graveyards and you'll see dates on gravestones that go back as far as the Famine in the 1840's. Make it a point to talk to some of the old people you meet about their past, and don't forget that they too were young like you in strange and hard times. What we don't realise is that during the Famine over a million people emigrated and at least one million died of starvation.'

Matthew liked this idea. It was the kind of project that he and his friend Pat could do.

'Right class have a good holiday, take care and I'll see you back here in September.'

'Matthew we'll look into our family tree to keep him happy. When we check the graveyard we might find out something about his ancestors that will shock him.' Pat started to laugh.

'That's a good idea. Maybe we'll make a discovery that will surprise him and us as well. There's one discovery I'm definitely sure we'll make Pat.'

'What's that Matthew?'

'That everyone in the graveyard will be dead.' He laughed saying. 'At least I hope they are.'

On his way home from school Matthew would have to pass down by the church, where he'd drop in for a few minutes. Then he'd head across by the Furley pad, better known as the Mass path, towards home. On his right hand side he noticed high up on the hill, the rock that Finn MacCoul had thrown there. According to legend he was a giant and judging by the size of the rock he must have been in a bad mood Matthew couldn't wait for school to finish so that he could get a job and become independent.

Having his tea one evening, his father said to him.

'Matthew we cut some barley for Pete Brown today.

The Bluebell's Mystery

He asked me would you go down at the weekend and give him a hand to put it into stooks. That's providing the weather stays good for the next few days.

Pete was a bachelor farmer who lived alone and like most of the farmers he had to hire help to save his hay and barley.

'That sounds good dad. I'll make myself a few bob, at least I'll be able to go to the pictures and not always be asking for the lend of the money.'

'That will make a change,' his sister Teresa remarked, smiling.

He had three sisters and two brothers. Being the youngest in the family he got all the abuse, at least that's what he thought. It didn't occur to him that he got more favour than sorrow.

It was great weather for stacking the sheaves and he was happy working in the sun.

'Matthew in a while will you come up to the house and we'll have something to eat, then we'll put down a bit of straw in the shed for the cattle', said Pete.

'Okay, I'll see you up there after I finish off this bit.'

When he arrived at the house they had tea, and out they went to fix up the shed.

'Do you play football at all? This is how I used to play when I was at it.'

He shouldered Matthew and knocked him down. Laughing Pete came over to help him up and in doing so, supposedly accidentally, felt Matthew's private parts. Thinking about this Matthew became wary but said nothing.

'You're very strong for a young fellow,' said Pete, making as if to wrestle.

Matthew could feel him push himself hard against his leg and alarm bells rang in his head, he knew there was something wrong.

'You caught me by surprise that time,' said Matthew laughing, pretending he didn't notice anything strange.

With a big smile he waited for Pete to come at him again. His youth allowed him to sidestep Pete's advance and he tripped him, glancing round he saw him lying in the straw, shocked, no smile.
'Ah-ha I caught you that time,' said Matthew. He was gone by the time the old goat arrived out. He was not paid for his work and he never went back near the old codger. He knew there had to be something wrong. All his thoughts were about girls but he'd heard that some boys and men were attracted to the same sex. Matthew knew the boys were right when they used the word queer. The incident made him wary for the rest of his days, and he told his brother about the incident.
'We'll stay away from that old dog, let him and his barley rot in the field.'
   Putting this incident to one side of his mind, Matthew and his pals carried on with their adventures. One of these he'd never forget. It was a strange encounter of a kind.
It began at a small lake named Lough Phouca. It was so deep it was frightening to stand at its edge and look in, even though they could swim. The water was perfectly clear and they could see right down to the bottom. The river ran across to the caves, a weird spot, dark and cold. Before entering the caves it flowed underneath the rocks.
'Do you know lads I was told that when Cromwell was in Ireland he was supposed to have executed men and women in this place. It's said that the people came and hid in the caves to get away from him. He lit fires at the entrance so that the smoke went in and choked them
'On account of that I'm inclined to think that this particular place is haunted,' said Pat.
'It's terrible to think that people were killed here isn't it?
Matthew thought, it's wild and lonely, the kind of place a boy and girl could spend time together and feel as if they were away and all alone, a lover's hideaway really.

They wandered round behind the caves to see where the river re-emerged to find little hideaways that had a lot of rocks covered in moss, they pulled it back to see millions of ants.

'It's as if we're God,' said Michael, 'looking down on millions of mankind going about their daily chores, strange isn't it?'

'Keep moving lads, I'd leave those creepers alone if I were you,' said Peter, 'they'll sting the arse off you.'

The river emerged from underneath the rocks with an endless gush, into a lovely green-banked, wide, shallow flowing flood of water. But of course it had to be contrary as it went underneath a curved hedge of blackthorn.

'Going through this ditch is going to give us a lot of cuts,' said Michael.

It was worth it to see the green carpet covered in bluebells.

'Hey lads, come in here look at this,' Matthew shouted.

The bluebells ran down and across to the river and up on the far side. The laser light glistened through the hedge, the gentle breeze made the light look as if to shiver, a magical ring came from the bluebells as they would quiver, it set an imprint on Matthew's mind that would last forever. A stone at one side was a nice seat to sit and watch this scene.

'You sit down over there Matthew and rest your lazy arse, we will look for the treasure,' said Jerry.

Matthew watched as the sun's rays darted across to catch the flowing stream and glisten on the water. He sat and watched its beauty, and the beauty of some of the girls that haunted his mind. Sitting here dreaming, he imagined a girl moving along as if floating on top of the bluebells. He looked around for his pals, and he realised he was on his own dreaming, he thought of Cromwell and ghosts. A fear crossed him, but it could not lessen the beauty of this place.

'Come on lads let's go,' he heard the call, he had a last look at this magical haunting place. Perhaps sometime in the future he might get back he thought, he knew he'd never forget being here.

Chapter 9

Mary and Teresa became friends and did confide in one another. Going about their work, tidying up the dining room and polishing the silver ornaments. Teresa asked; 'When was there a ball here last, Mrs. Ward? Where you here for the last one, and do you think they will ever have another one?'
'There was one here about five years ago Teresa, there are rumours going around that there is going to be one this year. It was rumoured last year too. We'll just have to wait for it to happen if it ever happens.'
The older ladies, who were here for the last ball, described to the girls the beautiful styles of the wealthy ladies. From the descriptions they gave, Mary was wondering did these ladies cover themselves at all. According to these women they wore lovely clothes, lots of jewellery and shoes that laced right up past the ankle. As usual this would spark thoughts in Mary's head of special designs of dresses.
She wondered if she were to make an effort to design and make a dress, who would wear it?
'Teresa I have an idea,' Mary shouted as she wiped the dust off the top of the dresser that stood along the dining room wall. She loved to clean the little crevices of the fancy woodwork and then polish them with beeswax. This brought a lovely shine to the dresser and a beautiful aroma. Handling the ornaments, some from countries like India and Pakistan made her nervous, so she treated them with great care.
'No doubt some kind of a crazy idea Mary, knowing you.'
'It's not that crazy. We should start now and make two ball gowns as if there is going to be a ball in six months time. If it happens all the better, and if it doesn't we'll

wear them ourselves to the ceili and that will open an eye or two.'

They could see the smile on Mrs. Ward's face. She was thinking to herself here they go again with their daft ideas, but they do put a lot of good humour into the work place.

'Do you want to give the priest and the local people a heart attack wearing low cut dresses like that to a ceili,' Teresa smiled. 'Why don't we draw a few sketches and we'll see which ones look best.'

'You know it's a long time since I sketched anything. I used to draw when I was helping my father fishing down by the lake.'

Between the laughing and talking they created four or five different designs. Some of them were tight around the hips with low necklines that would shock the male population. They all had skirts down as far as the top of the shoes, and one of them had a frill almost tipping the ground. Oddly enough it was the long tight-fitting dresses with the low cutaways at the neck, short sleeves and some of the shoulder exposed, that the ladies liked most.

'Whichever of you girls drew these sketches is good at art,' said Mrs. Ward. Someday I'll get you to do a sketch of me. It's a pity I didn't know you girls when I was younger.'

'I'd say you were good looking in your younger days Mrs. Ward.'

'Yes Mary I was as good looking then as you two girls are now. Ageing is the process that wears youth and beauty away, isn't that right?'

'You know Mrs. Ward that saying is very true and those words have deep meaning.'

'Sure we were all good looking in our youth. She smiled and made her way back to the kitchen with her memories of yesteryear.

'Those girls are talented,' she said to her friend Alice. 'If the design and the quality of their dressmaking is anything like their art, then they've got it all.'
'The way you talk about those girls tells me that they should not be working as housemaids at all.'
'Yes you're right Alice, no doubt, time and circumstance, will dictate their road in life.'
This was an evening to be remembered, if not for the dresses then for the laughing and good fun.
'Did you hear Mary tonight quoting her little poem?'
'Oh! Yes, it was good it went something like this:'

We will make them dresses,
We'll make them for the ball.
We will make them dresses,
Make them for one and all.
The ladies we will really thrill,
With fashions so good looking,
The men will chase them round the room,
And try to take them courting.

The idea of making a special gown perhaps two appealed to Mary.
'Ladies,' said Teresa, as she started getting the potatoes and carrots ready for the dinner. 'We're going to need some material. If we go about things the right way people won't know that some parts of the dresses are made from old clothes.'
Peeling a turnip and slicing the onions she had collected from the back garden, Mary wiping the tears from her eyes looked at Alice and said:
'I think that if we could pull off something like this it would be a miracle.' She put her hand to her mouth and yawned, the tiredness was starting to show. Early mornings, working all day, dressmaking in the evenings had them exhausted. The antics of the two girls did not go unnoticed. Helen Melen having heard all about their ideas from a spy in the house carried on

as though she knew nothing, although she, like the other ladies suffered from curiosity.

'I'm delighted to be going to this ceili on Friday night Mary. We do need a break.' Teresa sounded tired.

'I agree with you. One of my brothers will be there and I'll go home with him for the weekend.'

'Be optimistic Mary, you might meet a handsome fella and sure maybe he'll see you home.'

'Optimism is the word.' They laughed. After a good night at the ceili Mary made her way home.

Her mother was delighted to see her. She explained all about the big house and particularly the ballroom.

'Can you imagine being at a ball in a place like that Mary, with all the lights lit and the different colours of the dresses? The orchestra playing waltzes and you dancing with your boyfriend.'

'Yes Cathleen, our minds can take us on a tour of a wonderful scene, handsome looking men, beautiful styles, attractive looking girls and a mood that brings out the best in everyone, along with the laughter the merriment the happiness. Oh yes, wouldn't it be wonderful?'

'Come on Mary let's pretend we're at this great ball right now, dance with me.'

'No I'm sorry sir, I'm not dancing with you, I'm dancing with my friend over here. Come on mother, let's dance.'

Their father was quick to take down his old violin and started to play. Soon the family, were having a party.

'Well how are you getting on in Melen's these days Mary?' Peter asked as he danced her round the kitchen floor.

'It's not a bad place to work at all but I must say they do keep us busy.'

'I'm sorry I had that row with you just before you started work there, I was wrong.'

'That's alright Peter, I understand.'

The Bluebell's Mystery

They laughed and reminisced and stayed up until tiredness took them to bed. Having breakfast the next morning their mother said:
 'You know that Cathleen is getting married soon.'
'That's great, have you set a date yet Cathleen?'
'No we haven't, you'll be my bridesmaid won't you Mary. We'll have a ball just like the one we had here last night.'
   This news started Mary wondering about herself. What strange road would life take her down, would she have a hard life? Was she to go down life's road alone, or meet someone she really liked? Perhaps 'love' that was a hard word, a word she was afraid of, because it had too much deep meaning and feeling. She felt sad leaving home to go back to work. She was thankful when her mother said. 'I'll walk down the road with you a bit, sure it will do me good.'
On her way Mary was aware of the colours of the countryside, the quietness, the loneliness and the wildlife. She was also aware that all this belonged to them. It seemed to her that God had arranged that we should stand back and admire its beauty. From the top of the hill she viewed the roofs of the houses on both sides of the main street. She could see the road ahead of her it seemed a long distance and she wondered would she ever make it that far.

Chapter 10
Matthew

Stepping out of this magical circle Matthew said.
'Let's go over to that old house Pat, it looks like it's been there since the famine times. We'll check it out, we might even find out who lived there. Don't forget we have to keep our teacher happy.'
They made their way over and gave the ruins of the house a thorough inspection, noticing the cow dung on the floor near the old hearth, the rusted swing rail that was still over the fire. The doorway into the back room was crumbled to pieces.
'Look at the stone slabs on the floor Pat. People were poor back then, weren't they?'
'We think we're badly off now but it must have been terrible in those days.'
Matthew sneezed three times in a row. Pat laughing shouted. 'God you must have a 'flu coming on.'
'I feel a bit dizzy, I'll sit here on this old stone seat for a while and you go and check out the back for treasure.'
Matthew closed his eyes and felt his head spin. He imagined someone close to him. He felt as though he was floating in the air.
Suddenly he could see a white cottage with a thatched roof and a half door, on the slope of a hill that ran down to the curve of the river. Matthew was standing on the slate floor the fire in the hearth was lit with some sticks and turf. The burning turf and timber brought a pleasant feeling to the kitchen. He could see there was a ceili on. A man sat on a stool in the corner playing a fiddle, another man sat close to him playing a tin whistle. The men entering through the door would lift off their caps and say. 'Hello, good health to all here.'

Then they'd sit down and have a drink. A few young ladies entered the house and said good evening. Matthew was included as one of the guests. The girls and boys danced to the music. He could see that this was not his time, yet it held a pleasure that he could not understand. It was a time of great poverty, that he could see from the style and the dress of the men and women. Yet for all their wants, joy and laughter showed through. Seeing the old slate floor again told Matthew his brief encounter with the past was gone. Pat arrived back into the room.

'I feel as though I was at a ceili way back in the old days.'

'I'll give you a word of advice Matthew.'

'What may I ask would that be.'

'When you go home take a few tablets for that 'flu you have, and then jump into bed for about a week.'

'I'll do just that Pat but now I think we should get to hell out of here. I think this place might be haunted.'

'Anyway it's a derelict old dump now isn't it?'

'Derelict is the word for it, the only thing this house has going for it, is that bush of roses growing out the back. Did you see them Matthew? I'd say they were looked after back in the old days.'

They caught up with their pals at an old house, that had to be inspected for treasure.

'Let's light a fire. This house needs warming up and so do I,' shouted Pat, slapping his arms to warm himself.

'We'll look for the treasure. You light the fire your self.' Michael shouted back at him.

A jackdaw's nest started burning, and it raised so much smoke it almost choked them. They found a gun and a few empty shells and what they thought was a real bullet. They assumed the revolver was real because the firing pin was pointed. The cap guns they were familiar with when they were younger had flat firing pins for banging the caps.

'We're going to have to test this gun lads, that's a real bullet.' 'Look at that,' Jim held it up and showed it to the gang.

He inserted the bullet into the gun with curiosity.

'Careful Jim don't wave that thing around, if it does work you could accidentally shoot one of us,' he heard from one of the boys.

'But maybe it doesn't work,' he said smiling, as though he knew all about guns, 'we must test it.'

'Right if you are going to test it, then why not try it on the dog.'

'We'd better ask Michael first if that's okay, it's his dog you know, said Tony.'

'Hey Michael we're not sure if this gun is real, can we test it on your dog?'

'No that's not fair, why can't you test it on a bottle or a tin can.'

'I have an idea Pat, get that bit of old board. It's fairly clean, just pick up that lump of clay and put a bullseye in the centre of it.'

He stood the board against the wall saying. 'There's your target, now see can you hit it, you idiot.'

They still wondered had they found a real gun. If so then this was major treasure.

'It's not going to work,' said Pat, dithering a little. 'Bang!' the noise stunned the lads. Jim let the gun fall. 'By God Jim that was a mighty shot, said Tony, you nearly hit the bullseye but why did you let the gun fall?'

'It kicked back and nearly broke my hand. It's heavy you know.'

'It's a pity we haven't got a few more bullets then we'd really be great shots.' Pat laughed.

'Yes! and that noise will be heard all over the country and it will bring the guards down on us, and right now that's the last thing we need.'

The Bluebell's Mystery

'Look at the size of the hole in the timber.' Pat shouted, 'imagine putting a hole like that in a man, he'd surely be dead.'

'That would have killed one of us you know.' Jim sounded afraid. 'If you'd aimed it at the dog he'd be dead now.'

Matthew sounded thankful, he turned to the dog saying. 'You're lucky to be alive do you know that.' He patted him on the head.

'Anyway lads,' Jim shouted out. 'I think the best thing to do is to leave the gun back and tell the guards where it is.'

'That's a good idea and we'll give them a right good telling off for letting people leave guns lying around.' The boys had to laugh at this.

It seems that the gun belonged to an old man, dead now, who had returned from America. He must have brought it back with him.

Negotiations of great importance were made by the boys to go home and eat, and all meet again tomorrow.

That evening Matthew heard that he and his pals nearly burned the house down. Tiredness overtook him. He dreamed about his wanderings, his ghost girl, and of course one particular girl he fancied at school. She was good looking, he thought, not realising that all females looked good to him at his age. To a boy, she had all a girls, mysteries and attractions. She'd be the centre of his dreams tonight school was soon to finish. Thinking of the day's events he decided that tomorrow he and Pat would look into their family tree.

Chapter 11

At the end of what seemed a long journey Mary was glad to step into her place of work and was greeted by Helen Melen.

'Hello Mary, how are you this morning, I hope you had a good weekend. I was just telling Mrs. Ward and the ladies, that we are going to have a week of celebrations in three month's time. There's going to be a lot of people here. Sometimes I wonder should we be bothered with these parties at all.'

Mary was delighted to hear this, but she could also see that Mrs. Melen was getting anxious.

'It will be a great time for you, all the fuss, people, horses, carriages. Yes madam, you should enjoy those days, riding round the woods, boating and fishing and meeting all the people. They are your friends you know.'

Helen was surprised at her reply and could see an enthusiasm in Mary, rather than the indecision of her more mature self.

Mary's mind instantly thought this was a chance to show off our dresses and see what people thought of them. If they like them good, if not who cares, at least we will have tried.

They put a lot of effort into getting everything ready, cutting, stitching, matching colours, spending hour working hard. Finally the time came for them to show off their designs.

They marched round the room modelling their creations for their friends. The ladies were called on to give their unbiased opinions. The dresses were similar in style, slim fitting around the top part of the body. One dress had four straight pieces from the bodice to the hem, under both arms and one at the front and back. These pieces flared out at the bottom to suit the curve of the dress just above the shoes. The dress was white with a red matching frill around the hem. It looked attractive. The second dress was also low cut, in what two young people of the time considered respectable, even though they had stretched decency a little. This caused laughter amongst the ladies.

The spy in the house had done her business, so Helen Melon decided she'd find out what was going on.
'Mrs. Ward I'd like you to tell me what exactly are Mary and Teresa doing? Are they doing their work all right?'
'Oh yes Helen, those girls work very hard and they are no trouble whatsoever. At the moment they are playing with designing dresses.'
It was due to Helen's conversation with Mrs. Ward, that a knock came on the bedroom door while the girls were modelling. In order not to let the girls, know that she was suffering from curiosity she said: 'Ladies I'm glad to have found you all here. We are going to have to hire more temporary staff.'
As she talked she noticed Mary parading across the floor modelling her dress.
'That's a most unusual dress Mary. It has a lovely cut about it. I like the way it sits on you, it shows up your figure.'
'Do you really think it's nice? We made the one Teresa's wearing as well. We're experimenting with unusual designs.'
'Unusual is the word, give me a better look and turn round. Yes, that dress looks pretty. Well thank you girls for your attention.' Helen had satisfied her curiosity.
After getting over the shock of being caught modelling by their boss, the girls biggest problem was, to find out who might be going to the ball and might have the nerve to wear their dresses.

'I'm going for a walk Teresa, Mary said picking up her coat, do you want to come along?

'Yes I will, the fresh air will do me good.'

As usual they discussed the boys and whether or not they would go to the next ceili.

'That lad from school you went out with Mary, will you go out with him again?'

'I don't know, I'd like to meet someone different.'

'Look at the ducks and the swans, they just sit on the water and float - they don't have problems like us Mary.'

'Mrs Melen didn't say much to us about the dresses but she did admire them, so maybe they're better than we think they are.'

They stood and watched the birds for a little longer. They admired the trees, and the green of the shrubbery, the birds heading home. The girls turned and faced this huge domineering castle and quietly headed back, each wrapped in thoughts of their future. Where was life going to take them? It was a time of freedom and anxiety. Tiredness and bed were calling and before long it would be morning.

Helen on her way downstairs from the modelling exhibition reminisced on her past. It brought her mind back in time to when she looked young and pretty. Wearing one of those dresses with her slender figure she'd have won the day with the men, and shocked the ladies. She recalled the times she had in some of the great houses in England. These young ladies are making special dresses. It's their turn now I'll leave them alone. She could see similar traits between herself and these girls when she was around their age. She was reared in a small town in Hatfield, Hertfordshire.

Her brother Daniel acted as her minder. He had a lot of friends, she liked it when he brought some of these boys home, and she'd get to meet them.

'Daniel I was invited to an engagement party over in my friend's house this weekend; it will be all right if you bring your sister,' said his girlfriend Sarah.
Helen was delighted when Daniel agreed to bring her along. At last the great night came, and she saw the ladies in their lovely clothes.
Her green dress with its striking white top and a shawl over her shoulders made her look pretty. Her fair hair was neatly combed close to her face. A silver chain with a little brooch looked just right around her neck.
She had a few dances before her brother arrived over to her with one of his friends.
'Helen, I'd like you to meet this friend of mine.'
'Hello, my name is Ted Melen,' he said smiling.
He was about her age they danced and enjoyed each other's company.
'Will you have a drink with me,' he said.
'Yes I'd like a cup of coffee, please.'
She saw he was fairly tall, slim built and handsome. The music stopped, and in a courteous manner he excused himself.
Her next few dances passed without incident, but her mind was on this fellow. He appeared again and asked her to dance. She was shy, but she felt great when he said that he would like to see her again.
"That would be nice,' she said.
'I'll be coming down to see your brother soon.' With that he took his leave and said goodnight.
This was the beginning of a romance that led to her marrying Ted and coming to live in Ireland.

    The Fridays came round quickly and Mary went home to visit her family. Talking to Cathleen, Mary could see she was getting anxious about her wedding.
'Things are not going too well just now, the landlord is pressing Jim's father for more rent. He sent out Mr. McCoy, he's the wicket dog working for the landlords and he terrifies people.'

'Don't worry too much Cathleen, all those problems will sort themselves out after you're married.'
Mary was wondering what the future held in store for her when she heard Cathleen call.
'Mary, let's go over to Jim's farm and I'll show you where our house is going to stand. It will be just here on the side of the river and it will replace this old derelict building that looks as if it's been here for a thousand years.'
'You know Cathleen this will be a beautiful place to live.'
'When the sun is shining the ripple from the river will give an endless shimmer to one's eye, and we'll be able to see a constant gleaming silvery line going on and on,' said Cathleen.
Mary was feeling sad. This place gave her a feeling of security and belonging. She wondered would she ever know what it was like to belong.
They walked at their leisure towards home.
'How is the dressmaking coming along?' This question started Mary laughing.
'Wait until you hear this Cathleen. Mrs. Melen caught us modelling our dresses.'
'What was her reaction?
'She said they were unusual but nice.'
'It's strange she should knock at that particular time isn't it Mary? There's a spy in the house I'm thinking.'
'Don't you know there probably is. Mrs. Melen is all right. She was pleased with the dresses and she's the kind of lady that urges you to do things. She notices your abilities and doesn't resent you in any way like some people we know.'
Arm in arm they arrived home. Their mother had the fire lit, the house was warm and the kettle hung over the fire. They were greeted with the question. 'Would you like tea ladies?'
'Of course,' they replied, and now the giggling began. There was a relaxed atmosphere in the house and in a

carefree way each went about their chores. They sat and talked about younger days, coming home from school, people they knew, where had all their friends gone, who got married to who, where did they live? Mary heard some of her school friends had gone to America.
She thought this conversation was painting a wonderful picture. Could these stories be true? Her mind took her on some wonderful romantic trips to this strange place. Perhaps herself and Teresa would go there and make all kinds of new designs of dresses? This thought brought a smile to her face.

Her father stepped in through the door.
'Hello Mary how are you and all over at Melen's Demesne?'
"Their all fine, how are you getting along father?"
'Ah sure there's not a bother on me, did you hear that old Paddy McCabe died, other than that things are grand.'
Her weekend passed quickly. As she walked to work she remembered her first morning going through this part of the country. The fox, the rabbit and now the birds were whistling and singing as if they were attending a celebration. It was a lively scene to see. Looking down across the valley, a green patchwork quilt, she stood and enjoyed the beauty of this scene. Thinking about life's road, she soon arrived at Melens.

Chapter 12
Matthew

As they walked out towards the old graveyard Pat said: 'I thought you were going to take Breda Kelly with you Matthew.'
'We'll collect her on the way.'
Written on a stone at the entrance to the graveyard was the year 1798. It brought memories of their history classes. This was the year of the great rebellion.
'Pat this is history at its best it's not just classroom stuff.. The people in these graves were just like you and me, God it seems so long ago.'
Pat held Breda's hand and talked about the names on the tombstones, as some of them were still standing.
'See the name Murphy on that stone, it's the same as yours Breda. Maybe they're relations of yours, so we'll make a note of it.'
'That one over there has the name John McCabe written on it. He could be a distant relation of yours Pat'
'Do you realise,' said Pat pointing at the gravestones, 'that most of the names in this graveyard are from around here.'
'You know something, that's very observant of you, where the hell did you think they were from, America?'
'There's no need to be so smart-arsed Matthew, keep your smart remarks to yourself.'
Breda started to titter at them arguing.
'Well whoever is buried in that grave in the corner made sure they took their roses with them, didn't they?'
In a fearful kind of whisper and laughing Matthew said. 'Maybe he came back one night with a spade and planted them himself. Did you ever think of that?'

The Bluebell's Mystery

Pat walked over and pulled a rose and handed it to Breda saying; 'They smell nice don't they?' Taking the rose from Pat, she smiled and blushed.
'When we tell the teacher what we found here, he'll be happy with us.'
'Do you know Pat that some of these people here were the parents of the people who died in the Famine.'
'It must have been a terrible time. We'll never realise how bad it was.'
'Imagine in a country like this people actually died of starvation it's hard to believe.'
On his way home Pat left Breda to her door. He was shy in her company.

Matthew worked part-time in a sawmill after school. He didn't like it when he had to help cut down trees. He would be told by his boss to insert a wedge in the sawcut and give it a wallop with the sledge. The tree leaned forward with a frightening crack and it sent a shiver down Matthew's spine.
'Let's saw a little more, now hammer the wedge again and when you hear another loud crack, check which way it's going to fall and run like hell.'
It was terrifying. At first Matthew liked the work; his boss was a bit of an inventor, who came up with some good ideas. It was great to see that due to his inventions it was so easy to load the heavy logs.
When Matthew finished school he stopped working in the sawmill and went to work in a quarry. It was a job he didn't really like. However it kept him at home and this suited him.
'Matthew,' the foreman shouted, 'get up on this bulldozer and I'll show you how to drive it. Now clear away the soil from the top of the rock.'
This took a couple of days. He liked driving the big machines. When the topsoil was cleared, he was sent to get out the compressor and the drill. He had to drill holes and fill them with dynamite. He was learning how

to handle explosive devices and he got to be a bit of an expert in this field, a fact that did not go unnoticed in certain circles. He thought that while it was quite dangerous working in the sawmill and cutting down trees, it was twice as dangerous working in the quarry with explosives.

The foreman was a pleasant man, there were two other fellows working there, Frank and Seamus, he was a bully. Matthew could see that Frank, was being bullied by him.

'You're not supposed to be driving that digger Matthew,' Seamus said in his usual sneery way.

'If you have a problem with that then take it up with the foreman.'

Seamus looked upset. Here was a young fellow giving him cheek and he didn't like being treated the way he treated people. One day he called Matthew a nickname.

'You're not to be calling people names you bully boy. Surely you can see that it was you and you're bullying, that caused Frank to leave.'

The drilling of the rock took a long time it was slow work. Some of the holes were a lot deeper than others. After two days drilling they were about to start filling the holes with dynamite, when four men dressed in masks and carrying guns walked into the workshop.

'Stand against that wall or we'll blow your heads off,' said one of them, pointing a revolver at Seamus. They took the boxes of dynamite and hurried off saying: 'Make sure that you don't tell the guards anything about us, do you hear.'

It was a threat that was heeded. This incident shocked the bullyboy and everyone else.

'You didn't suck up too much to those boys Seamus,' one of the lads sniggered, Seamus wasn't impressed.

After this incident the company was obliged to call the guards whenever they were blasting. When the police met Matthew they recalled the incident with the revolver when he was with his pals on one of their adventures years earlier.

'Listen lads we want to know your names and addresses,' said a guard.

Matthew knew he'd always be under the eye of the police because he had access to, and was able to use dynamite. Due to this, he realised he'd have to change his job. On his way home from work one evening at a quiet place along the road he was stopped by two men.

'Matthew, we heard you are good with dynamite. If we were to ask you to make us some explosive devices would you do so? We use them occasionally. You probably heard about us on the T.V. or radio. Can we persuade you to work with us?'

'Ah no gentlemen I don't think I'd be able for that type of work.'

He was shocked that they had asked him at all.

'You know Matthew,' said one of them, 'this conversation never took place, is that alright with you?'

'Yes it is indeed gentlemen, we never met.'

Chapter 13

'You think we're busy now Mary don't you, well imagine what next weekend will be like, when the celebrations start.'
'To be honest with you Teresa I don't give a damn, the celebrations don't bother me at all. What does bother me is, will we get the dresses worn? To make that happen I'd work day and night.'
'Mrs. Ward told me we'll have to get the empty rooms upstairs ready for the guests, Mary.'
'Come on then we'll move quickly and get them done before she knows where she is. I think that woman's up in a heap, all this is too much for her.'
Although it meant everyone worked harder, the anticipation of the festivities put a buzz into everything. The humour in the workplace was good and the ladies discussed and wondered what the style would be like.
'I was told by Evlin that the dresses the ladies will wear will leave plenty of room to show off the string of pearls and the golden or sometimes diamond jewelled brooch.'
'Isn't it amazing Teresa, the way some people have so much and others little or nothing, sometimes not even enough to eat.'
'These are the gentry, they have everything except of course the dresses we made.' The girls laughed.
'I wonder how will they feel when, we show them our styles.'
'I'm sure they'll be thrilled,' said Teresa, sounding doubtful.
Working in the kitchen the following day, the girls began to walk around as though they were modelling. Mary, holding a plate up high, twisting the upper part of her body and shaking her backside and playing the part of a grand lady said.

'What do you think of my dress ladies?'
They walked and shook their bodies in sexy ways, twirling round shaking themselves in outlandish movements. It was a time when everyone relaxed, none of them realised they were being watched from above. It was a charade that lasted about half an hour. The girls would put on a fancy English accent and go, 'La Dee Da, La Dee Da,' while laughing.
'We can be just as hoity toity as these ladies,' said Mary.
Helen Melen watching from above walked away with a smile on her face thinking to herself. 'I'll give those two, something to be hoity toity about.'

Over the next few days they saw some strange looking carriages arriving, some had one horse others two. Alice walking through the kitchen said. 'I think this is going to be a right big party girls.'
'I remember the last time there was a celebration here like this,' said Mrs. Ward. 'You young girls will see a lot of foreign people who are not from around these parts at all, people from England and all over Ireland and other parts of the world.'
'If you keep your eyes open you might meet an English man,' Alice smiled.
Mary didn't like this woman as she considered her the kitchen witch. She didn't like doing the menial jobs like washing dishes and pots or peeling spuds. Instead she liked to be around Mrs. Ward, licking up to her.
Mary and Teresa met some of the guests and the strange accents gave them a laugh. Some of them behaved in an aggressive grand important manner. The staff noticed and just tolerated the bad mannered people. However, the people with normal manners were treated with more courtesy.

'Look at those people Teresa getting out of that carriage, notice the way they are dressed. Aren't they really well off? Just look at her shoes, they're lovely. Would you like to own clothes of that quality?'

'Of course I would, but I don't think you or I are going to be in that class and if we ever get there it will be a miracle.'

'Ah Teresa, don't forget that sometimes miracles do happen.'

'Have a look at that young man who just got out of that other carriage, do you see the way he's dressed?'

'He's a handsome looking chap isn't he Mary?' 'He's alright but if all the lads at the ceili were dressed like that, wouldn't they be a handsome bunch?'

'It will be a treat to see these people when they are dancing at the ball.'

'We'll approach Mrs. Melen and ask her up straight would she persuade some of the ladies to wear our dresses and if she doesn't well that's it, to hell with the whole situation.'

'It's worth a try Teresa. It's probably our only chance. It would be a pity to miss this once in a lifetime opportunity wouldn't it?'

'While we have a bit of idle time now we'll go for a walk, it's a nice day.'

On their way they met a few gentlemen and a girl down on the lawn. One of them turned saying, 'Hello ladies do you work up at the castle?'

'Yes we do.'

'Are you over for the celebrations?'

'Yes we are, this is a lovely place isn't it?'

They noticed the English accent.

'I don't suppose there's any sense in us asking you two girls out,' said one of the men. 'Perhaps a walk through the woods this evening, or maybe go out on the lake in a boat?' he smiled broadly.

'Thank you for asking us but we must refuse your request because Mrs. Melen would frown on such a gesture on our part.' Mary giggled. They could tell which fellow was with the girl because he held her hand, but both of them agreed all three were handsome. Under normal circumstances they would have dated them but again the word English crossed their minds.

As they turned to walk back towards the house they stood perfectly still as a pheasant walked towards them and then turned in no hurry to show them an array of colours of such beauty they could hardly believe their eyes.

Mary looked at the castle wall, its domineering height made her feel small and insignificant.

'Did you ever wonder what life is all about Teresa? Where is God? Who is God? Does he know us? Where in heaven's name do we fit into all this?'

'To be quite honest with you Mary, I don't think too deeply on those things. Thinking so deep would drive me mad.'

Mary thought of how well she had got to know Teresa Boyle and how good a friend she had become. She also wondered was she going to stay working at Melens for the rest of her life. If she had a boyfriend what would he be like? Would he be someone from around this part of the country, would he love her, would she love him, what was love, would they have a happy life together, would she have children?

'Teresa do you ever dream of having lots of wealth, land, horses and a big house, a life of ease and comfort with servants.'

'I have Mary but it's something that we cannot afford to dream about.'

This reply brought Mary back to reality. She laughed about that wonderful life but real life was different, although it was nice to dream once in a while. She decided it was best to let circumstance take its course. Influence it yes, but in the final analysis it's what will be will be. The crow's squawk overhead told them, 'to go home and go to bed that's where we're going,' it said. They stepped through the door and shivered, it was chilly outside. They went to the kitchen and had tea with Mrs. Ward.

'Well ladies I think it's time we went to bed.'

They entered their bedroom and looked at the folded dresses again. Morning arrived too soon. They went about their duties with enthusiasm after a good night's rest. Mary was busy washing potatoes for the dinner in the kitchen, Teresa had been sent upstairs to get the bedrooms ready for the guests. Looking out the window she saw a carriage pulling up to the front door. Later she approached Mary saying, 'I saw a most unusual carriage this morning. It was completely closed. It had four big wheels and two horses. A young man and his girl stepped out of it. You should have seen their style! She was beautiful in her long dark coat, black hair held up by a diamond clip. Her boyfriend was dressed in a three-quarter length coat, a white shirt with a black bow and I must say he looked handsome.'

'I hope to god Teresa, you're not throwing you eye on some Englishman. If I did that my brother Peter would go mad.'

'Her dress looked a bit like the ones we made but I must say not quite as tight, and even if I do say so, not as nice. We'll shock everybody if we can get someone to wear them, Oh, but it would be great.'

'I think Mrs. Ward is upset at us Teresa, she's making us do everything.'

'No, she's not upset at all, it's just that the place is getting busier.'

Every time they went to the kitchen there seemed to be extra staff about, everything was moving faster, they didn't realise the celebrations were so close. Friday night is the first dance, then a rest night and then the great ball on Sunday night. After that the guests would just drift away over the next week or so. The two girls were becoming disillusioned with the whole dress debacle. Later that day taking her courage in her hands

The Bluebell's Mystery

Mary approached Helen Melen with a determination to solve the problem once and for all, and said:
'Mrs. Melen will you do us a favour please, and show some of the ladies the dresses and ask them will they wear them just to show them off? If they don't like them well so be it,' she was almost crying.
'That's a good idea Mary and I think I know two young ladies who might just wear them. I'll let you know.'
The girls were delighted and so happy that work didn't seem to matter. Later that night they took out the dresses again and modelled them around the room for each other, checking if they were perfect in every way. They didn't realise it but the dresses had become a part of them.

Chapter 14
Matthew

Being young adventurous and optimistic, Matthew decided it was time to leave Carrick. He tried but didn't succeed in getting a decent job, so he headed for Dublin. He wanted to see what city life was like. With anxiety and anticipation of great things he turned and said goodbye to his family. He picked up his travelling bag and walked the mile into town to catch his bus. Passing the Ballybay cross roads he stopped to look down at the bright sun on the corn. He watched the sun as it chased the shadow across the field, the breeze bending the barley. It was the weight of the shadow that made the barley bend and shiver as though it could feel the cold. The sunlight raced down the valley towards the workhouse and up the hill on the far side - the brightness, the darkness the sandy colour of the grain rolling like the tide before him. He stood in wonder at its beauty. Looking at this scene, he knew it was something he'd never forget. It gave him a great feeling about the beauty of the earth and the country he lived in. This was Ireland in the nineteen sixties. Standing here now he recalled how he used to watch this scene on his way home from school. He remembered the poet's words. The stoney grey soil of Monaghan, the County of the little hills. He realised how times change and this might be the last time he'd ever witness this magical wonder of nature's beauty. He could feel the heat of the sun as he made his way to the bus and on to a new adventure.

Some hours later, after travelling through the country and noticing the historical significance of places like the Boyne Bridge and Slane Castle, he arrived at the bus depot in Dublin. From there he telephoned his friend who would give him temporary accommodation. Having a few hours to spare Matthew walked as far as O'Connell Street. There he viewed the architecture of the GPO. He made it his business to enter this particular post office and buy a few stamps. This building reminded him of what he learned at school about the 1916 Rising and the men who died in that battle for Ireland's freedom. When he came out onto the street he stood and appreciated the grey coloured stone of Clery's store on the opposite side of the street. On his left stood Nelson's Pillar, a monument to Lord Admiral Nelson. He climbed the steps to the top of this great tower and from there he viewed the city. He could see the full length of O'Connell Street as far as Parnell Square where a monument stood to Parnell another one of Ireland's great men. Over the rooftops he could see on high ground Guinness's Brewery. And down to his right he could see O'Connell Bridge with the statue of Daniel O'Connell standing with his angels, some of which had taken bullets during the 1916 Rising. These were just a few of the historical sights of Dublin.

Matthew liked the city. Instead of having to walk everywhere all he had to do was jump conveniently on a bus, it was a big change from travelling on a bicycle and getting wet as he made his way home.

   He got himself a job in an engineering fabrication shop in Santry. After a few weeks he took new lodgings in an old house that was being refurbished. His bed-sit was on the top floor. He hated coming back late at night because he was the first and only tenant in the house. When he would open the front door, the darkness and the silence brought great fear. The door would close behind him before he had time to switch the light on. Looking towards the back of the house he was able to see the sky. The back door blew open in the breeze but he was scared to look in that direction. He thought there was a pair of eyes watching him. When the door behind him closed on its own, he wondered was it the breeze or was it something sinister? He was terrified trying to find and press the light switch on the ground floor, because then he'd have to run half way up the stairs and press the second switch before the first light went out. Once the light came on he felt safe. He was so nervous he knew that if he did not make it to the second switch, he'd be set upon by something weird, a spirit or a ghost.

After a while the room across the way was occupied. Matthew met the gentleman on the stairs one day.

'Hello I'm John Murphy.'

He seemed nice enough, being tall and slim and he wore a black polo neck shirt, with sleek black hair and a black suit. Was it possible he could be the devil? Thought Matthew. He'd have to get in control of his fear.

'You and I are the only people in the house you know,' said Matthew. 'I sometimes hear strange noises at night, do you?'

'That's odd, I haven't heard anything,' said John laughing.

A lady moved into the flat at the landing level. She opened her door one evening to ask a question. Matthew noticed the holy pictures on the wall.

'Hello, are you the tenant in the top flat on the right?'

'Yes I am.'

I'll introduce myself, I'm Lily Martin.' Matthew saw her black hair was turning grey and could see by her style that she was around the same age as one of his older sisters.'

'My name is Matthew O'Neill, I was the first tenant to move in here. It seems our landlord is re-furbishing this house from the top down.'

'What's the strange noise I hear coming from the landing in the middle of the night - did you ever hear it?'

The Bluebell's Mystery

'Yes I heard it and I'm glad to know that I am not the only one, as I find it weird. Sometimes late at night I feel cold and afraid, although I haven't seen anything.'
'Perhaps it's all just imagination,' she smiled and invited him in. He noticed the crucifix and a little bottle beside it. He thought of his mother and the holy water she put in his bag when he was leaving home. Looking at the holy pictures and thinking of the things this lady spoke about, he knew he'd go for his bag as soon as he left her.
'I keep my door locked at night Matthew I'm afraid to open it.'
'What are you afraid of?'
'Those strange noises and the strong bright light that shines under my door,' she replied.
The noise on the landing woke Matthew one night. There seemed to be a terrible coldness in the room. He prayed and fell asleep. Next morning it was as if nothing had happened. He spent his day wondering about the strange noises and was terrified of going back to his flat. You need never be afraid of the dead he was told when he was young by his mother. Consoling yes, but what about evil spirits?
'You know something Patrick,' he said to his friend at work. 'When I'm going back to my digs late at night I get the feeling the house is haunted.'
'Has it ever occurred to you Matthew that maybe it is, just think of the time the British were here. The 1916 Rising and all the murders that took place - I wouldn't be a bit surprised if it is haunted.'
'I'll tell you something strange that happened to me once Patrick, you'll have a good laugh, but this is strange.'
'This should be good, let's hear it.' Patrick smiled.
'I had a dream one time when I was a young fellow. I was going home along the Bottley Lane behind the courthouse in Carrickmacross, where the tower is on the right hand side. When I came to the end of the lane

I looked over a farmyard gate into a graveyard. The strange thing about this is that there never was a graveyard there. I could see gravestones and one particular headstone stood out dead clear. It was an odd kind of dream wasn't it Patrick?'
'Yes it was unusual Matthew. There's just one question that needs to be asked about that dream.'
'What's that?'
'Whose name was written on the gravestone? Was it your name by any chance and did you see the date?'
Patrick began to laugh.
'No there wasn't a date or a name.' This started Matthew thinking.
'Maybe there is a ghost in that house you're in. The point is, will you frighten the ghost or will it frighten you? Maybe someone in the house is doing strange things like devil worship or playing with an owiegi board. Maybe they're talking to the other side, perhaps even to evil spirits?'
Matthew didn't like this kind of talk. It didn't help the situation, even though Patrick was only making fun of it. The lady living on the second floor seemed to be nervous. The gentleman across the way didn't say anything, yet it was on his landing everything weird was happening. Matthew arrived back to his flat late one night. He turned the key and pushed the door open to see a light at the top of the house. He relaxed. Quietly he crept up the stairs, not needing his usual two lights. He sneaked a glance across the top landing, this allowed him to look into John Murphy's flat. It was as bright as the sun. There was a beautiful girl sitting on the bed in a very evocative position with her long hair covering the top part of her body. John was standing in various positions taking photographs of her. So that's what it's all about thought Matthew, smiling. He went to bed and slept soundly.

At his work the next day he felt as though all his problems had been solved, he knew now his fear was just imagination. However, a different type of fear returned when he was asked by the manager, Mr. Clinton to step into his office for a few minutes. 'We have a job to do in Galway. Will you go down for us Matthew?'

'Yes I will.'

He was delighted to be going to another city. He often heard people talking about Galway and now he had the chance to see it for himself. Getting away from his lonely flat and the fact that the Company would pay his accommodation made him feel good.

This was a great job to be sent on . . . new places new faces, he checked on all the dances. He headed off to a dance in the Seapoint dancehall in Salthill where there were three men for each woman. He overheard a fellow ask a girl: 'Will you dance Jane?'

'Sorry Pat, I'm already asked.'

'Well can I have the next one?'

'I've promised that one as well.'

Matthew thought to himself, don't ask her again. Sadly enough, he did. After hearing this fellow being refused so many times, Matthew was nervous. However, he ventured across the floor and asked a girl to dance, but before she could refuse, he gestured his hands outwards and said: 'No! No, I'm sorry it's okay,' surprisingly she said yes.

He enjoyed dancing with her. She was a good dancer and she was an attractive looking girl. As usual he'd say: "There's big crowd here tonight."

'Yes much bigger than usual, I think most of these men are over from the mines.'

He felt in their conversation they were getting on well, and between the dances they stood talking. He knew it was going to be hard for any fellow to get his mark off tonight, just too many blokes.

'Would you like to go for a mineral?'

'Yes okay,' at this they laughed.

Sitting down, her question came. 'What part of the country are you from?'
'I'm from County Monaghan.'
'I don't know that part of the country because I've never been up there.'
'You mean to tell me that you've never been to see the stony grey soil of Monaghan? You must have heard of Patrick Kavanagh, one of Ireland's great poets.'
'I heard some of his poetry at school but I forget it.'
'What part of Galway are you from and anyway what's your name?'
'Marie Finnegan and I live just about a quarter of a mile from here.'
He noticed her blue dress was straight down, low cut around the neck and it clung neatly to her body, showing all her curves. How lucky can a fellow get? All these fellows here and I win.
'Come on Marie, let's dance again.'
He put his arms around her and she allowed him to move closer. He felt her body against his. He forgot all about the crowded hall.
'Would it be okay if I walk you home tonight?'
'Yes that would be alright.'
They arranged to see each other again, kissed and parted. He thumbed a lift back to his digs but it left him that he had to walk five miles in the rain.

Working in the crusher the next day Matthew heard the shout. 'Everyone, get outside quick!
He turned to see the heavy smoke and the flames rising towards the ceiling, the fumes were beginning to choke him. One of the workers, welding and burning overhead caused the rubber to catch fire. This set off the ear-piercing sound of the alarm. There was great commotion, with fire brigades and police, and people running in all directions. The bloke who started the fire was pointed out to Matthew. He was from Germany and seemed cool about the whole affair. Why wouldn't he, thought Matthew. All he had to do was jump on a plane

and vanish. He didn't realise that his setting fire to the crusher caused Matthew to be sent back to the big smoke and away from his country girl.

Chapter 15

The knock on the door signalled morning.
'We're going to have to start going to bed earlier Teresa.'
'I agree with you but we say that all the time and it never happens.'
They made their way down to the kitchen, and were met by Mrs.Ward who said in an anxious fashion.
'There are about two hundred desserts to be made, Mary will you do that job?'
'Yes I'll start them now.'
Mary began by getting the apples and the dough ready. The apples were sliced and put onto the cooking pans and slipped into the oven. It was nice working in the kitchen the smell of the food cooking and the heat made it comfortable.
'Teresa you get those potatoes ready will you?' She pointed to the basket of potatoes on the floor.
Teresa was shocked to see the amount of spuds she had to peel. She glanced at Mary who was smiling. The other ladies were making sandwiches and getting the vegetables and the cutlery set out. Time was marching on and the guests were arriving. Looking at some of the carriages, the girls could see the horses had their manes combed and they looked handsome.
Alice, looking out the window remarked.
'Some of the men arriving in those fancy carriages look nearly as handsome as the horses.' It brought laughter.
It was an easy time to be working, because something different was happening all the time and the ladies were calling to each other.
'Look Mary, see this for a fancy wagon?'
Between the working and the watching and the activity the time flew in. Dinner was served to almost one hundred and fifty people. The kitchen staff were run off

their feet, very soon it was time to serve the dessert. The apple tart and cream looked delicious. There was plenty of wine to drink and the cigar smoke could be smelt everywhere.

'You and I will sneak up to that little balcony tonight Mary and we'll watch the guests dancing,' said Teresa

Mary was thinking the dresses would fit the good looking girl that Teresa told her about.

At last the dinner was over and it left a mountain of washing up to be done, but when all the ladies leant a hand it went quickly enough. Most of the guests wandered out and around the grounds. They walked about the lake, watching the swans and ducks. Some people went boating. The staff slipped up to the top of the castle to see the style of the guests. Although it was a nice mild evening, after a while a chill crept into the air. Collars were seen pulled up, the walking and boating slowed down, and people stayed in and enjoyed a drink.

'Look the musicians have arrived, Mary. Very soon we will be working to the sound of music.'

'Ladies, it's time we started to serve the drinks,' said Mrs. Ward.

'When do you think Mrs. Melen will allow our dresses to be worn Mary?'

'I don't think it will be tonight.'

After a while Jennie turned to Teresa and said in a low tone. 'There's something strange going on in the ballroom. I was serving drinks to some of the guests and even they were wondering what was happening. A lot of people were leaving with Mrs. Melen and heading towards the room at the main entrance.'

'We'll soon know what's going on, because we're bringing them drinks now.'

They were shocked when they arrived with the drinks to find everyone had left the ballroom.

'Something strange must have happened to cause everyone to leave Teresa, let's hope to god that the celebrations are not called off. There was a great chance Mrs. Melen might get our dresses exhibited here tonight.'

'Wouldn't it be just be our luck Mary if the whole thing was cancelled?' They mingled with the guests as they served the drinks.

'Let's not be pessimistic Teresa, this is only a dance and a feast here tonight, so let's hope it happens.'

'Although we don't like the penny-halfpenny snobbery of some of these people, we'll enjoy ourselves. At least we'll make sure we get the best of the food.' said Teresa.

Laughing Mary said. 'This apple tart is fit for a king. I'll have a piece, although it's unlikely I'll ever be a king.'

Some of their friends who were serving drinks came back with stories that they'd seen some of the guests wearing masks.

'You were here on the last occasion Mrs. Ward. Was there ever a masked ball? I think we're going to see one tonight,' said Mary.

'If it does turn into a masked ball nobody will know anybody so it could be a lively weekend yet.'

'Mary, you take that tray and bring it to Mrs. Melen and her friends in the guest room.'

In the far corner sitting at a table, she saw Helen and her husband, an attractive looking young lady and her handsome boyfriend. Seeing them there laughing and talking and enjoying each other's company made Mary feel sad. She felt inferior and badly dressed. She consoled herself with the fact that if she had the same clothes as that girl she'd look just as good. She wondered would their dresses be a match for this kind of style. Her only consolation now was that when Mrs. Melen asked these girls to wear them they could refuse, and this could save the day for Teresa and herself. Mary was getting disillusioned

The Bluebell's Mystery

'I'm fed up with the whole escapade, so if it doesn't work to hell with it,' Mary said to Teresa back in the kitchen.

Her thoughts wandered back to the young man she'd seen in the guestroom. His fair hair was combed neatly back. He wore a high collared shirt with a red cravat. He was about her age, and as he spoke to his girlfriend she noticed his smile. When she was serving their drinks he said: 'Hello, thank you.'

Their eyes met for a brief moment, he smiled and she blushed. As she turned to go she could see that his girlfriend had noticed their close exchange of glances. Was it just her wishful thinking, or did he really notice her?. She fantasised and allowed her mind to dream romantic ideas about him.

Later when she was having a cup of tea, and eyeing a nice cream cake, Mrs Ward approached her and said. 'Things have changed tonight Mary. While it started out as a ball, some bright spark decided it should be a masked ball. That's what Helen Melen told me.'

'Well that should make things interesting.'

'There's one other thing Mary, she also said that she knows two girls who will wear your dresses.'

Mary jumped up from her chair. 'That's great news Mrs. Ward. I'll go up and get the dresses ready.'

'That's a good idea Mary and take Teresa with you. Put on your dresses because you two are wearing them to the ball.'

In shock Mary sat back down on the chair and wiped a tear from her eye.

'It being a masked ball, Helen told me that when you and Teresa enter the ballroom, nobody will know who you are.'

Mary was thrilled yet afraid when she heard this news. Now she felt that she and Teresa had to do, what they had hoped to do, but now having to do it, Mary was afraid.

'There's something else Mary, when the two of you are dressed, come down to the kitchen. I'm going to arrange with one of the stable hands to borrow a carriage. He'll pick you up and bring you to the front door, where you will be announced. Do you know Mary that Helen Melen is as anxious as we are to see if you girls can pull this off. She's enjoying the bit of intrigue.'

'You won't believe what I was just told Teresa,' said Mary, full of excitement.

Teresa standing holding an empty tray could see tears in Mary's eyes. 'Did something happen? 'Mrs. Melen knows two girls, who will wear our dresses.'

'Is that right?

'Mrs. Ward told me to collect you, go to our room put on our dresses, Teresa you and I are going to the ball.'

They got ready in a panic. The ladies from the kitchen were as excited as the girls were. They offered to help them in any way they could by giving them various pieces of jewellery, lipstick, pearls, anything the girls wanted the ladies got them. It seemed that this was more than a mere ball for the Irish ladies, it was a competition between the well off and the poor. The style of these grand ladies and their wealth, against the ideas of two girls who had nothing and who's ideas was going to be paraded here tonight.

When they arrived down to the kitchen the staff admired their style. They noticed Mary's red hair and her long flowing dress. Her laced up shoes with slightly tinted brown leather.

With their make-up and jewellery the girls looked stunning. The young man, who went to get the carriage was amazed at their good looks. He went round to the stables to get the horse and carriage. Having been introduced to the girls, he spoke to the horse in a whisper saying, 'let's go horse.'

The ladies stood and watched the girls and made little remarks.

The Bluebell's Mystery

'With a wave of their arm they'd say, 'My Lady,' to Teresa. This laughing and banter went on for a while, yet there was anxiety and fear about everything going all right.

Mrs. Ward allayed their worries when she said:

'Girls when it comes to style and beauty you need have no fear, all you need now is to have confidence in yourselves.'

They entered the coach with tension, holding on to each other.

'I'm going to take you for a spin around the grounds and when I pull up at the door, put on your masks before you leave the carriage,' said the stable hand.

'How did we ever manage to get ourselves into this dilemma,' said Teresa.

A gentleman standing outside the main entrance opened the coach door and said. 'You are.'

Chapter 16
Matthew

Matthew didn't like leaving his girl behind in the country they felt sad having to part. However, he was happy being back in the big smoke where things were very much alive. Standing in Parnell Square amid all the young people going to the various dancehalls, Matthew and his friend were undecided.
'Which dance hall will we go to tonight Matthew?'
'I don't know Tony. Here, we'll toss a coin: heads we go to the National Ballroom, tails we go the Town and Country club.'
They both looked up as the coin twirled in the air.
'Heads it is, so it's to, the National we go.'
They liked this particular ballroom with its mirrors on both sides of the dance floor right up to the stage. At the end of the hall there was a little bar where they could sit and have a coffee. He planned to go down to see his girl in the country soon. He liked her and he felt guilty for not going to see her. The company was slow to send him back down and this led to problems for Matthew. He had met a girl in the city, who was good looking, loved to dance, go to the cinema, sometimes concerts. They went out and enjoyed themselves as much as possible... it was that time of life. Dine-wine-dance-romance. Yes, these were the times to live no doubt god had ordained this to be so.
One night sitting down over their coffee, Tony with a big smile on his face said to Matthew: 'The Botanic Gardens are holding their annual dinner dance on the twenty-third of next month. We can bring our friends with us. Why don't you ask that girl you're going out with Matthew, would she like to come along? I've already asked Angela and we're going. Oh, there's just

one other thing you should know Matthew.' He started laughing.
'What's that Tony? Don't tell me it's going to cost me a hundred pounds?'
'To hell with the cost; I'll lend you the money if I have to.'
Matthew realised then that Tony was a good friend.
'It's a dress suit affair.'
'Do you mean I have to wear one of those monkey suits, with a dickey bow?'
Tony started to laugh loudly, saying: 'You'll look great!'
'Anne might not want to go to one of those dances with me Tony, I don't know her that long.'
'Ask her anyway, sure girls love that sort of thing. I know she'll accept, you'll see.'
Matthew met his girl on the next Wednesday evening. After leaving the cinema he took her to a café for coffee and a cake. He studied her looks. Her hair was short and a dull blonde colour, curled down and combed close to her face. Her nice complexion and her smile caught his gaze.
'Stop staring at me Matthew. People will think there's something wrong with me.'
'I wasn't staring Anne I was just noticing your good looks.'
'Now you're trying to flatter me Matthew. Is there something wrong? Are you going to work in the country again?
'No I'm not, but there is something I want to ask you.'
'You sound serious, what is it?'
She took a spoonful of her apple tart and cream. 'This is lovely,' she smiled.
'My friend Tony as you know works in the Botanic Gardens. He wants to know would we like to go to the annual dinner dance with him and his girl? I'm going to have to wear a dress suit and a dickey bow.'
She started laughing loudly at the fact he was more concerned about the dickey bow than anything else.

'That's great, of course I'll go. Where is it taking place?'
'In the Gresham Hotel on the twenty-third of next month.'
'Thanks very much for asking me. Now I'll have to get myself a dress and shoes.'
'It should be a good night anyway.'
Leaning across the table she whispered in his ear.
'We'll make it a great night,' she said, kissing him on the cheek.
The big night came at last. Matthew caught a taxi to her house and pulled up the collar of his overcoat to hide his dickey bow when he was invited inside.
'Hello Matthew is the taxi waiting?' Anne could see Matthew was conscious of his appearance and was doing his best not to be noticed.
'Yes it is Anne. He said he'd wait.'
She began to laugh saying. 'I notice you're keeping the collar of your coat pulled up.'
He smiled.
It was his first time to meet her family. Anne looked elegant in her satin green dress and a white stole over her shoulders. She wore a gold locket around her neck with earrings to match.
Matthew felt proud to be standing here with this nice-looking girl he'd only known for a few months. They entered the hotel where he could feel the softness of the carpet under his feet... something with which he was not familiar.
'Look at the size of the chandelier Anne, isn't it lovely? Look at the way the light glistens through the glass.'
'Yes, it is a joy and a beautiful piece of work.'
He enjoyed the elegance of the hotel, and the paintings on the wall of some of Ireland's great heroes and writers. He had been told this hotel played its part in the time of the 1916 Rising. They entered the ballroom and were ushered to the balcony on the right-hand side. This area was furnished with soft seating on both sides, with a square table in the centre. They had a

glass of wine while they were waiting for the dinner to be served. The mixture of wine and soft music caused a lot of tittering and set in motion an expectation of gaiety, dancing and laughter.

After a sumptuous meal they sat back and enjoyed the remainder of their wine. The music soon took them to the dance floor, where various spot prizes were on offer. The glamour and the style, on the dance floor, was eye catching, it was a wonderful experience for Matthew and his girlfriend. After the joys and pleasures of that evening, life came back to normal again. They'd reminisce on this exceptional evening and hoped that they would be asked to similar functions, this being Christmas time.

They met under Clery's clock their usual meeting place. He saw her coming towards him in her white sheepskin coat with the collar turned high to keep the breeze away. He could see she felt the cold as much as he did.

'Come on Matthew, we'll go into that café and have something nice to eat and get out of this gale.'

They sat and talked and got to know each other better. After a time of going to the cinema and dance halls, he could see things was getting serious. His thoughts would drift between the two girls, always a dilemma.

Could it be that god was playing games with him?

'You know something Anne, you might think this a little strange but I'll tell you anyway. One time when I was at school my pals and I went on an adventure. We followed a river through the caves and strange things happened to me that I didn't tell them about at the time because they would have thought I was crazy.'

'Well come on tell me. I'll probably think you're crazy too.'

'Anyway, I saw an attractive girl floating across the bluebells and I thought I saw fairies. I spent a long time listening to them playing music and it was strange and lonely. I'll tell you Anne, I put my thoughts of that incident into a rhyme.'

'It will be no harm if you tell me what the rhyme is.'

He thought that she would consider him a bit of an idiot but he'd say the rhyme anyway.

'You see Anne I wondered:'

Did God send the fairies down, he did you know He sent them down to find us,

He sent them in our hour of need, when our foes were here to grind us.

We'd see them in the quiet places, mostly just by chance,

As yet, they had not seen us, watch them, sing and dance.

We called them the fairies, at first it was a joke,

Sometime later on you know we called them, the wee folk.

They had a secret weapon, gold, they'd tease us with its sheen,

But we had a secret weapon too, we called it poteen.

It was a drink they couldn't handle, it was great to see them drunk,

To see them slip and slide around, up to their eyes in muck.

'I asked myself afterwards how much time did this take and did time stop for that length of time? All this made me wonder,' he said.

She smiled at him. 'Perhaps you had a 'flu Matthew? Were you, on any pills or medicine, or did you take any alcohol? Anyway I'm ordering another coffee, would you like one?'

After six weeks in the city, Matthew decided it was time to go home and see his family. Having a cup of tea

with his sister she asked: 'How are things in Dublin, and do you like it up there?'
'I do Teesie. My mate's dinner dance was in the Gresham Hotel last week and I brought my girlfriend.'
'Well I'm going to tell you something now that you don't know about the Gresham.' She started to laugh.
'What is it then, tell me.'
'That's where mam and dad had their wedding reception.'
'I didn't know that when I was there, but it's quite a posh place now. Is there anything happening in the town tonight that I should know about?'
'Yes, there's a dance in the Catholic Hall. I heard the girls at work saying there's a good band playing. I don't know what's on in the cinema, but Kate might know.'
The nagging pain in his tooth told him he'd better visit the dentist first before he went anywhere.

Chapter 17

'Ladies your names are?' The footman bowed with a sway of his hand and ushered them towards the main door.

'Mary and Teresa,' they answered, as they stepped down from the carriage.

'Welcome to the ball ladies. You may have a drink in the guestroom before you enter the ballroom.'

A glass of wine relaxed them. As they walked along the hall they saw the shining floors and the gleaming mirrors, and it reminded them of the hard work and effort they had made to make this place as beautiful as it was. Their entrance to the ballroom showed them an array of colours they had not seen before. The lighting from the candelabra gleamed through the mirrors and gave a pleasant aura to the colours in the ballroom. Their entrance from the door to their table caused heads to turn amongst the guests. When they got to their seats and saw the beautiful styles of the ladies and gentlemen, they relaxed, knowing that nobody could recognise them because of their masks.

Helen Melen enjoying her drink with her husband and sons smiled at the charade that had just taken place. Little did any of her family or guests know that the two young ladies, who had walked the length of the ballroom and were a great attraction to all, were members of the kitchen staff.

Mary was asked to dance by a smartly dressed young man, she was thrilled. She could see this was going to be a good night. After a while they were served tea by one of their girlfriends. In a low voice her friend said: 'Ah yes your tea my lady,' to Mary, 'Ah yes your tea my lady,' to Teresa, they had a laugh.

Helen Melen knew them by their dresses and wondered was it their style that had them dancing all the time.

'Look at the clothes here tonight Teresa. Isn't it great just to be at this function and enjoying the antics of these people?'

'Look at the way the young men are dressed Mary, with their long coats and high type collars, their shirts with their cravats. I like their waist coats and shiny shoes... they do look handsome don't they?'

'You know Teresa, we're here to show off our dresses not to look at the fellows.'

'I suppose you're right but they are the ones doing the looking and the asking.'

A tall young man approached Mary and he shyly said. 'Would you like to dance?'

Mary thought she saw him earlier in the guestroom. She was sure he was the young man that she had seen with the good-looking girl in the red dress. With his mask on now, she could not be sure. She felt shy, but if it was him, why was he dancing with her? She could see he was young and about her own age.

"Are you enjoying this party tonight?'

'Yes the music is good, What do you think of it being a masked ball?'

'I think it's great that you don't know me and I don't know you,' he smiled. 'The dress you're wearing is nice and I must say, so are you. I'm not quite sure if it's the dress that makes you look beautiful or you that makes the dress look beautiful.'

This compliment caused her to blush. As they danced around the floor, Mary could see the light shining through the haze of cigar smoke, while the jewels on the ladies glimmered.

He escorted her back to her table. She felt thrilled yet disappointed that she might not get to know him better.

'Hello, how are you doing, are you enjoying the ball?' He said to Teresa as she sat drinking her coffee.

'I am indeed, it's a great night.'
'Thank you,' he said catching Mary's eye. This set her mind thinking there was something about him- she liked.
'We get to wear our dresses Teresa, I meet someone nice and realise I won't get to know him because of the masks, there is always a problem.'
The girls were aware that their pals were watching them from the little balcony above, and at times they'd wave to them. Their friends talked about how wonderful a time Mary and Teresa were having. They spoke of the whole thing as a once in a lifetime adventure, something that could never happen again. The music, the dancing, the style, to be a part of it just for this one night must be wonderful, and it gave the girls a thrill to think it could have been any of them. The excitement of the dancing and their awareness of the part they played in this elegant charade left Mary and Teresa tired.
'May I have this dance?'
She was shocked and thrilled to see the young man again - at least at a glance she thought it was him.
As they danced he asked. 'Will you be here for the ball on Sunday night?'
"I am not sure,' Mary replied.
'I'll be here myself. It will be a good night, if it's as good as tonight. I must say that dress you're wearing has caused a few people to wonder just who you are and where are you from.'
'Ah - ha, but this is a masked ball and I don't have to tell you anything.'
'Well you could tell me tonight because I'm going to find out on Sunday night anyway.'
'Okay we'll wait until Sunday night, then I will know about you and I will also know who your girlfriend is. I see you don't spend a lot of time dancing with her. Won't she be a bit peeved to see you dancing with me?'

He didn't answer this question. She thinks Sandra is with me, so she has noticed me, perhaps I should try and ask her out. No, I'll wait until Sunday night. 'Just to clear the way a little my first name is Tim.'

'Well I suppose first names don't really matter, mine is Mary.'

'Judging by the colour of your hair and your accent you must be from Ireland. Would I be out of order if I were to call you an attractive Irish colleen?' This made her blush.

They didn't realise it but in their messing around with what one thought they knew about the other, they had danced two sets, and it was time to part. Courteously he stepped back and smiling said: 'Thank you Mary, I'll see you Sunday night then.' She half nodded, knowing she would not be here.

'Mary who was that fellow you danced with twice?'

'Did I really? He asked me who I was but I didn't tell him. He said he'd see me here on Sunday night.'

Teresa turned and said, 'but we won't be here.'

'I didn't want to tell him that.'

They quietly slipped away without being seen, back to their workplace, and this sneaking around started them laughing. Morning had them wondering had they been in bed at all. Mary went to the tower to watch the guests on the lake. The swans drifted along with their heads bent low as usual. She noticed the pathways going down towards the lake, each bend leaving one to wonder what was hidden round the curve. She took time to think of all that went on last night. When they walked into the ballroom all eyes were on them and the ladies noticed the style. The masks were a gift that added mystery to the whole escapade and it was a night she'd always remember. Who was this Tim fellow she wondered? He had an English accent and yet at times he sounded Irish. She'd talk to Teresa about him and they would try and find out who he was.

'Mary I was talking to some of the guests in the ballroom last night and they asked me if there was any entertainment in the village. I told them about the tavern and the ceili on Fridays.'
'Can you imagine Teresa all those people heading into a tavern. Wouldn't there be a great demand on the beer?'
'You know a lot of people made comments to me about the dresses we were wearing Mary. One particular lady said she noticed us when we walked the length of the hall on the way in. She said it was as if we were modelling the styles, what do you think of that?'
'That's good news, at least she was an intelligent woman Teresa. Did you by chance tell her that's exactly what we were doing? I told that fellow I'd be here Sunday night and I won't, that's bad news.'
'Did you see the girl he was with?'
"Yes she looked nice in her red dress.'
'And he was trying to ask you out. It makes you wonder about these fellows.'
This little comment set Mary's mind wondering.
'Wouldn't it be a right kick in the backside to him if we were to find out who he was?'
'He's hardly worth bothering about.'
This remark made Mary feel sad because she liked him and she had hoped to see him again.

Chapter 18

As arranged the O'Shea's arrived at John Curtis's farm. It was a dull overcast day with such a cold breeze blowing that it would peel the skin off an apple. The clothes they wore found it hard to keep the cold from the body. They were joined by the Henderson lads the Dowds and a few other neighbours in the evening. Everyone complained of the cold. John called them into the house. They sat close to the turf fire and had a drink, which instilled a little warmth into them.

'As you already know men there's going to be a fair in two weeks time and it has been decided that we are going to need a few more cattle and anything else we can lay our hands on. As well as that there's a couple of families going through a rough time. I heard that they are barely able to feed themselves. Now we know we had enough of that during the Famine years.'

'Don't tell me,' shouted Tom. 'The reason these people are half starved is because some of the bastard landlords demanded animals or foodstuffs in place of rent money?'

John Curtis quickly replied.

'Sure don't you know they did, aren't they the cause of the trouble? I've been told that in four days from now a policeman's daughter is getting married to one of the landlord's sons. No doubt there will be celebrations afterwards and gentlemen we'll celebrate by moving cattle. Melens will not be the host farm this time. The animals and everything else will be taken from, as he likes to be called, Lord Admiral Dunathy.'

'Isn't that where Jack McCoy works as a game warden? He's a bad boy.'

'That's right Tom, you've heard about him no doubt.'

'I did indeed, he gave me a thumping out there in the field. If we're going up there we'll make it our business to try and teach him a lesson, alright.'

'The cattle will be walked along the Mortha road, which is about four miles long. James, you and Tom will meet the Henderson lad. If there's any danger at all, the hedges on that road have lots of gaps, so just drive the animals into any field and keep on walking and the cattle will just be strays.'

'Tom you'll be herding the cattle, and I'll walk about six or seven hundred yards ahead of you,' said his father.

He turned and said to Peter. 'You walk the same distance behind him. We'll have whistles with us so if you hear this noise Tom, you'll know the police are near.'

True to form four days later they headed to the Dunathy estate and there they waited and watched for Jack McCoy. As he entered the main gates they pounced on him and pulled a hood over his head. He let a roar as his cap fell onto the ground and exposed a completely bald, head. They tied his hands and pulled the rope round his waist to lead him along, and they told him not to make a sound.

With a disguised voice one of them said. 'Feel the bumps on that stick Jack. Remember if you make any noise, you'll get a crack of this across the head. It's time you learned that you are an Irishman. You must stop abusing your own people.'

Looking at McCoy from behind Tom could see he was a broad built man about six feet tall, he looked and fitted the part of a bully.

Tom was glad to give him a good hard kick in the backside. He led him off towards the cattle further into the estate and occasionally rubbed the blackthorn stick against his neck to keep him full of fear.

Some of the men made their way to where the sheep were held. Three sheep were caught. Two of the men held up the sheep, another man slit its throat and butchered it. Each man headed across the field with a slaughtered animal on his back.

'Jack, tell me now, where the grain is stored or you'll get a blow.'

He felt the stick against his head just above his eye.

'All right, take me around to the back of the house and I'll tell you. There's an old shed over there in the corner and that's where the grain is stored.'

Two of the men went into the shed and took a sack of grain each they put two more sacks on the donkey. They headed in the same direction as the men with the sheep. In the weeks to follow they would mill the grain and turn it into flour.

After what he thought was a long time, Jack was dragged through another gate. He was thinking these fellows, will kill me if I try to get away, and the landlord will probably sack me for not looking after the place.

The cattle were taken on to the Mortha Road as planned.

'Listen whoever you are.' Jack was pleading with his captor, 'while it looks like I treat the Irish bad, I do it in order to earn a wage for myself. If I don't do what the landlord says I'll be thrown off my farm. My wife's health is not good and that's the reason I can't afford to leave for America.'

Tom didn't realise that McCoy's situation was so bad.

'We didn't know you had so much trouble at home but to be honest with you, it's your aggressive attitude towards everyone that has us thinking you're a right bastard.'

'The reason I am so arrogant is because I'm trying to hold onto my job and while people see me as being wicked, nasty and mean, it's for show. The worst thing I've ever done to anyone was to give people a beating. By doing that I've been keeping the landlords and the Britsh happy, and sometimes doing that breaks my heart. So if you want to kill me, do it now.' He sounded terrified.

'Be quiet or we will kill you, just sit down on that stone and don't move,' he was warned. Jack didn't know that he was about one mile outside the village sitting on a stone outside Daly's house.

Tom took the end of the rope that was around his waist and tied it to the gate of the house.

'You'd want to be careful Jack. Don't move because if you fall off that rock you're sitting on, you'll break your neck. You're in a precarious position. As bad and all as you are and have been, we don't want to see you dead. Now, not a sound do you hear?'

There was complete silence for five minutes and Jack thinking that they'd left, started moving.

'We told you not to move didn't we,' the stick was dragged across his face again and there was silence. After a long time Jack began pulling the rope with his hands. The gate he was tied to moved and then swung backwards against the wall giving a loud bang. He kept doing this over and over and after what seemed an eternity, someone roared at him.

'What are you doing here Sir?'

The rope was untied and the hood was yanked off his head. He turned to see a young boy of about fifteen years of age beside him.

'Where am I?' he shouted.

'You're about a mile outside the village. I'm Patrick Daly, you know my father John. You're Mr.McCoy aren't you?'

'Yes that's right.'

'There's just been a robbery at the Dunathy estate and I might need you to tell the police you found me here.'

The young lad started laughing at the idea of a robbery saying. 'Did the robbers get away alright?'

'I think they did, that's why I was left here.'

Jack was thinking this young boy's explanation of things, might help him to hang on to his job.

Chapter 19

The celebrations started on Sunday night with the same pomp as they did on the previous Friday. Mary and Teresa were serving drinks and they could see it was going to be quite an evening. Not being part of this function tonight they'd enjoy listening to the music and looking at the grandeur of it all.

'Mary last Friday night some of these fellows tried to make dates with me. They even spoke about meeting me at the ceili. That means that all the people attending the ball are not from distant parts, so maybe someone recognised us.'

'You're forgetting we were all wearing masks, and anyway it doesn't really matter now. I have to hurry and take these drinks to the table at the end of the hall.'

While serving, Mary saw the handsome young man with his girlfriend. He stared, and she was conscious of him looking at her hair, so she smiled at him.

'Would you like me to get you anything else sir?'

'Perhaps later, thank you,' he smiled and their eyes met, while Mary blushed.

When she turned to the other people at the table, she could see they were aware of her. His girlfriend was watching her closely. Mary then glanced back at him. He was wondering where had he seen her before, or had he seen her before? His thoughts were interrupted when his cousin Sandra whispered to him.

'I think you're besotted with that girl Timothy, she's pretty ... she's almost as good-looking as I am.' This made them laugh.

'You know Sandra I think I met her somewhere before.'

His mother heard his remark and thought, little did he know The night's celebrations was enjoyed by the

guests. Helen was happy everything she'd set out to do had gone well, the partying was nearly over.
'Hello! Helen, can I have a word with you?'
The friendly greeting made Helen turn to see an old friend she knew from England walking towards her.
'Ah Marion Shelten, how are you doing, I hope you and your husband are enjoying yourselves.'
'Yes we are having a wonderful time and thank you for inviting us over.'
'How can I help you Marion?'
'As you know I'm in the clothes manufacturing and design business. I noticed two girls at the ball on Friday evening in unusual dresses. I don't see them here tonight. If you can see them before I go back to England, tell them I'd like to have a word with them.'
'Yes I know those girls and I'll tell them what you said. I'm sure they'll be happy to meet you.'
Helen was delighted, so the dresses were noticed and by a lady with the eye for style. Mary and Teresa will be thrilled she thought. She was happy to think that she was the one with the good news.
When Mary was leaving a drink on the Melen's table later on, Timothy ventured to say to her.
'Excuse me there's something I would like to ask you.'
'What is it sir?'
'I might be staying here for a few weeks and I'd like to know where I could go locally for a few drinks and a bit of entertainment.'
"Usually most of us go to the ceili in the village on Friday nights. You should come along and you might as well bring your girlfriend, as it's quite a good night.'
'Perhaps I will and I might bring my lady friend.'
'Okay I'll expect to see you there.'
Mary didn't know it, but Timothy and Sandra were amused at the fact that she thought the girl beside him was his girlfriend.
He began to wonder about this red headed girl. Should he, try to take her out? It's all right to have this bit of

carry on, because she thought he was with a girl. However, she did invite him to the ceili, so he would go even if Sandra did not.

He had never been to a ceili before, so it would be something new and it might be enjoyable. I'll claim my right as an Irishman by going and if I can I'll go out with this girl on Friday night - that would be an achievement.

His thoughts brought him back to last Friday night at the masked ball. There were two girls there in unusual dresses. He'd find out more about them. One of them seemed nice and she had red hair too. He'd ask his mother, she'd know their names. He remembered the one he fancied said she'd be here on Sunday night and she didn't turn up. In fact neither of them turned up.

At last Mary and Teresa got together and were able to have a good discussion before they went to bed.

'I told the young man about the ceili on Friday night, and I think he'll go.'

'Which fellow Mary?'

'The fellow with the good looking girl.'

'Well you are more or less obliged to be there. They won't know anybody don't forget they're English.'

'I'm going anyway, will you go Teresa?'

'Ah, yes I might as well.'

When they were having their breakfast the following morning Helen Melen walked into the kitchen saying sternly: 'I want to see you girls in your room at seven o'clock this evening,' and with that she walked off.

They looked at each other in amazement.

'There must be something wrong,' said Teresa.

'Well I don't think I did anything to upset her, so we'll have to wait and see.'

They did not know that Helen was playing a game. She was going to arrange with Marion Shelten to see them at that time. She felt good about this, so she let them think they did something wrong. When they realise it was about the dresses, they will feel great she thought.

Marion knocked their bedroom. Mary opening the door said 'Hello,'
'My name is Marion Shelten I'm a friend of Helen's and she told me where to find you.'
'What is it we can do for you?'
'I'm trying to find out where did you girls get the dresses you wore to the masked ball Friday night?'
'We made those dresses ourselves.' They started to laugh.
'But where did you get the ideas from?'
'I always had what I thought were crazy ideas in my head and of course when Teresa and I put our heads together we came up with the daft idea of it all.'
Mary picked up a few of her sketches and handed them to Marion.
'There's what made us decide to make them. It was for fun and just to see could we do it.'
'We asked Mrs. Melen could she get someone to wear them to the ball to show them off, and she surprised us when she allowed us to wear them ourselves.'
'Yes I saw them that night and that's why I'm here. I'm trying to find out what it was that inspired you to make them.'
'We asked ourselves the same question and the only answer we could come up with is, that the inspiration has always been in us and probably always will.'
'There's one other question I'll ask you. What exactly do you intend doing now girls? I'm in the fashion industry in London and I can see those dresses show a great flare for design. The fact that you had the ability and made the effort to take your designs all the way and exhibit them at the ball, shows a great energy. I'm giving you my address now and if either of you should decide to work in the fashion industry, then I'd be delighted to give either or both of you a job. So when you're ready just drop over and see me. Girls like you should not be working as housemaids, you should be

out there exploiting your talents. Now about these two dresses, are you willing to sell them to me?'
'Yes of course we are.'
'I'll give you one, no two shillings each, I'm going to take them with me and I want to know if it's okay for me to use them as patterns. I'm going to see will they create as much attention in London.'
'We'd also like to know, if they get much attention over there,' said Mary.
'I'll give you one more shilling between you to persuade you to come to London and work for me. What you must realise girls is, that circumstance has opened an opportunity, so now it's up to you to exploit it, and I can help. If you agree with what I have said, then give me your address. Now fold up the dresses because I'm going back to England to-morrow and I'll take them with me.'
'Thank you for your opinion on the styles, it's from someone like you that we needed to be advised,' said Mary.
Teresa quickly turned to Marion and said: 'Because of the things you've told us you've given us the drive to take our ideas as far as possible and no doubt, we'll start working for Marion Shelten in London.' She smiled.
Their discussion ended on a happy and optimistic tone. The extent of what had been said and the advice they were given would not sink in to their minds for a day or two. This had changed their outlook on life and it happened so quickly.

Chapter 20
Matthew

The dental receptionist was attractive, she wore a white coat with a yellow blouse underneath. Her curves and colours caught Matthew's attention so much that he forgot about the pain, but even her attractions were not enough to stop it.

'Hello, I need to see the dentist quickly,' he said, noting her smile.

'Just fill out this form and sit in the waiting room for a few minutes please.'

Thinking about the injection did not endear him to the dentist. He recalled some years ago at school when he was sent to the clinic. After having been given his injection he was called to have his tooth extracted, but his gum hadn't frozen properly. The pain caused him to start screaming. He didn't realise the dentist had to finish pulling the tooth anyway. It gave him a great fear of ever going to the dentist again. Thinking of this experience made him feel like going home.

He was called in, got his injection and was told to wait in the waiting room again. At least he could take his mind off this terrible pain for a while by looking through some of the magazines, which were full of good-looking girls. There was some kind of a modelling exhibition from London and New York. The ladies wore lovely clothes and some of the designs caught Matthew's eye. He relaxed a little reading about them. The door opened fear struck him, because he knew there was no going back.

'Matthew he'll see you now,' she held the door open for him.

He put on a brave face and in he went.

The Bluebell's Mystery

'Open wide,' said the dentist. After what seemed an hour of digging and scraping the ordeal was over.

'Will you sign here please?' she asked. He didn't have the nerve to ask her for a date. He'd try some other time if he met her. Right now he had to get to bed. After resting for a while Matthew went up to the kitchen for his tea. Not having been home in a few months he sat with his family around the cooker and talked of old times.

'How is the cat?' He asked his mam.

They laughed at how he'd sneak into the oven, someone would close the door, and eventually he'd crawl out again half roasted, and then stretch out as best he could on the cold concrete floor to cool down.

'You know we could have been charged with "cat roasting," and put in jail,' said his father. Everyone laughed.

Having the chat and getting ready to go out, Matthew was feeling a bit afraid because he might have to walk home in the dark.

'Do you remember when we were coming home from the cinema one night Peter. I was carrying the flashlight?'

'Yes I do, what about it?'

'When we came to the top of the hill, I saw a shadow of a man cross the road in front of us. I flicked the light, did you see the shadow?'

'No I didn't see anything.'

'Well I'm amazed at that because I did.' His father interrupted them saying: 'Do you lads know, that there was a Tavern on that hill way back in the eighteenth century and that someone was murdered there?'

'Yes I heard that story alright,' said Peter. But a lot of those things are only heresy.'

'I don't give a damn if you believe me or not but I did see something and I assumed that you had seen it too. That's why I didn't say anything to you at the time.'

Matthew was shocked that Peter hadn't seen anything. He had come that way on his own at night before and was always scared. Luckily nothing ever happened. Knowing he might have to walk home tonight made him wary. Maybe some of the lads will have a car and they'll give me a lift home he thought. He knew that if he met a girl at the dance he'd take home. Still, to go with a girl he'd take the chance. What a price he'd have to pay...she wouldn't realise the terrible cost she was to him. Because of her he'd walk home, ghost or no ghost.

Chapter 21

Normality began to return to the Melen household after the celebrations, although some of the guests were still around.
'I saw that fellow and his girlfriend down at the lake Teresa, so they must be staying on to go to the ceili. It will be interesting to see them there.'
'Maybe it's not wise for them to go at all Mary, considering the anti-British feeling of most of the young people.'
'We'll be there anyway and we'll make sure that we join them and that should make things easier for them. Anyway the boys will be more interested in her looks.'
'Maybe we should start now and make two more dresses,' said Teresa with a giggle.
'You know it's strange how things happen. My meeting you and our dressmaking, and that lady- Marion, she above all people seeing them. It makes one wonder, is it just chance or is their someone else at work here, destiny or god, it makes you think. What did you think of her offer of a job in London Teresa?'
'You know it's not a bad idea, Mary, working here at this kind of housework is not satisfying. It would be alright if we were married and settled down. Wouldn't it be great to go there and make crazy styles, doing the work we like best and getting well paid for it? It's something I'm thinking strongly about. At the minute there is no panic, right now I'll just think about the ceili.'
Mary went down for a walk around the lake a few times that week. She was aware of the bald coot flying across with its great wing span and its mighty flying power it was lovely to watch. There were two people out on the lake in a boat and she knew who they were. It was him, her fantasy boyfriend and of course his attractive girl.

The Bluebell's Mystery

It annoyed her when she was holding him close in her fantasy, his arms around her, but the thought of this girl spoiled things. She vowed that if they went to the ceili she and her boyfriend with the wandering hands would dance around them.

Eventually Friday night came. Mary and Teresa spent most of that evening getting ready. This night was going to be something special, so she knew she had to look her best.

When Mary was all dressed up she did not realise how well she looked. She wore her favourite pink dress before but she made some changes to it for tonight. The weather was soft and warm, she could feel the breeze caress her hair, and yes this would be a good night for a ceili.

Some of the older people came for the craic and a drink of poteen. The music brought with it a pleasant atmosphere, and urged some of the boys to ask the girls to dance. To see a carriage arriving was a most unusual happening at one of these ceilies. Two lads who worked at Melens jumped out and waved to people they knew. Everyone wondered and watched to see who else was in the carriage. A young man stepped down and everyone could see by his appearance he was from the well to do section of society. He held his hand out to help his lady friend. While he was noticed for the smartness of his dress, his girlfriend was noticed for her style and good looks. Timothy saw two men sitting on a bench at the side of the road. One played a tin whistle and the other a violin. Another man sat on a stool and played the accordion, and the foot-tapping music induced a compelling urge to dance.

'Would you care to dance?' The tap on the shoulder surprised Mary.

'Oh hello, yes I would.'

He noticed she was shy and as he danced with her he was thinking of her beauty. He felt shy in her company, but he'd make sure Mary did not see this.

The Bluebell's Mystery

'I see you both made it, did you have any trouble getting here?'
'No, one of the lads on the farm brought us over, and he said he'd bring us back to Melens tonight.'
His girlfriend who never seemed to leave his side was dancing with Eamonn, a friend of Mary's.
'My name is Timothy, what do you think of this ceili tonight?'
'It's very good so far. It's a lovely evening but we'll have to keep dancing or we'll get cold.'
'What did you think of the ball in Melen's?'
'That was a great night.' Mary laughed.
'You were serving drinks weren't you? I'm sure it was you I saw coming to our table. The girl who served the drinks that night was pretty but I must admit the girl I'm dancing with tonight is as pretty. The question I'm asking myself is, am I talking to the same girl?' He smiled.
Mary blushed. Timothy was pleased he had got away with his little bit of flattery.
Suffering from curiosity Mary asked Timothy.
'Did you go to the masked ball?'
'Yes I did and you know, I danced with a girl that night and she had red hair just like yours, she told me her name was Mary. Was it you?'
'Yes, it was, but we were not supposed to tell anybody who we were. Mrs. Melen allowed us to wear the dresses we made.'
"Ah-ha." so it was you and a friend who wore the fancy dresses. Who was the other girl?'
'That was Teresa Boyle...she's over there dancing.
 See that fellow dancing with your girlfriend. I went   to school with him.'
'That girl is my cousin. Her name is Sandra and she's not my girlfriend.'
'Oh, I thought she was!'
'Would it matter if she was?' Timothy smiled.

Mary, surprised and delighted replied: 'Not really,' she said laughing. He began to feel at ease. They enjoyed their dancing and didn't notice that the music stopped and started once or twice.
Sandra could see that Mary and Timothy were attracted to each other. It was as if there was nobody else at the ceili.

The thump on his back made Timothy turn around quickly to face a drunken fellow who was about to hit him. Timothy putting his hands out in a defensive way said: 'Can I help you?'
'No, you can't, I want to dance with Mary O'Shea,' he said in a slurred voice. Mary in shock said, 'Hello Dan, not just now I'm dancing with this fellow.'
'Oh sure, you'll dance with an English man all right but you won't dance with me. Well you'll dance with me anyway,' he said putting his arm around her waist and pulling her towards him. Timothy was about to push him away from Mary, when another fellow stepped in saying: 'Wait, a minute Dan. We can't be causing trouble especially with the O'Shea's, you should know that by now.' Putting his arm around Dan he said. 'Come on let's go, we'll get ourselves another drink.' Mary looking at this fellow, realised he was Patrick Dooley one of the brothers her dog left standing in the river. Patrick sat his friend down and returned to Mary. 'Can I speak to you for a minute please? You remember me, don't you Mary?'
'Yes indeed I do.'
'I must apologise for my behaviour towards you in the past Mary. Oh, there's something else, in two weeks I'm going to America with my family.'
'Thank you for your help tonight and mind your younger brother when you're over there.' They shook hands and he walked away.
Turning to Timothy Mary said. 'Patrick is a neighbour of mine, we were lucky he was here tonight.'

The Bluebell's Mystery

'Come on over Mary and I'll introduce you to Sandra.'
Mary was glad to shake the hand of the girl who caused her so much bother in her world of fantasy.
After the introductions and the bit of laughter, everyone enjoyed the evening.
Mary was happy to keep dancing with Timothy. She liked his manner, but he was not forthcoming with information about himself.
'How long will you be staying at Melen's?'
He realised she didn't know who he was.
'I suppose two or three weeks.'
'It was quite a weekend of celebrations, the two dances and now the ceili. You know something, you people really know how to enjoy yourselves. I've had a great time.'
The ceili was coming to an end, but he didn't have the nerve to ask Mary if she was going back to Melen's.
'Will I see you again sometime,' he said.
'Yes I'll see you next Monday because I'll be in Melen's at work.'
'I'll see you then Mary.'
She felt happy about the arrangement but was sad the night was finishing while feeling sorry to see him go. She knew she'd hear all about Sandra and the ceili from Teresa at work on Monday.

Mary made her way home for the weekend. Her mother was delighted to see her. She missed Mary and worried about her. Peter and Tom arrived home after a day's work at Curtis's.
'I heard you went to the ceili on Friday night Mary with your pal from work. How did you get on? I heard you danced with some of the lads that work for Melen's.'
'Yes I did dance with some of them and I also danced with everyone else who was there.'
'You and Tom missed a good night.'
She was anxious to get back to work. There was something she did not know about this Timothy fellow.

At least she would make it her business to find out who he was.

Chapter 22

Arriving at Melen's on Monday morning, Mary went about her work preparing the vegetables for the dinner.
'I have news for you Mary and boy are you going to be shocked.'
'Come on then Teresa, be brave and surprise me.'
'Okay then, your boyfriend is none other than Timothy Melen. How about that for a surprise!
'So that's why he was reluctant to tell me his name!'
Mary didn't want to get involved with these English people because she knew it would only cause problems in her life.
'Well Teresa it's like this. He said that he'd only be here for a few weeks, so I'll go out with him once or twice. He'll go back to England and that will be the end of it.'
'Sandra was delighted to have been to an 'Irish ceili' as she described it. She now has plans to go to the next one.' said Teresa.
'I think she has taken to your ex-boyfriend. You'd want to keep your eye on her.' This started them laughing.
When Mary met Timothy at the back of the castle on the evening as planned, her first words to him were:
'You didn't tell me your name was Melen.'
'I know, I must apologise about that.'
She was taken back slightly by his apologetic reply. She had feelings she didn't understand for this skinny young man who stood before her, in his slimline bright trousers and summer shirt. She liked his manner but she was wary because he was English. As they strolled along she saw the starlings, and indicated to him to watch. They swayed in the air as if they were doing a waltz, all in perfect rhythm with each other. They'd fly up, sway across, and then drop into the grass.
'I heard that you are attending University in England. What subject are you studying?'

The Bluebell's Mystery

'Civil engineering. I'll be finished in about a year.'
'What's England like?'
'It's just like here, but much busier.'
'When you finish school will you stay there or will you come back to Ireland?'
'I haven't decided what to do yet.'

Mary was watching all the activity on the lake. She saw a few men with fishing rods tying the boats to their moorings. She spotted a ball on the ground and instinctively she gave it a kick and they started to chase it. Laughing and pushing each other to kick it, the pulling and pushing unknowingly brought them into close contact with each other. He took advantage of this. At times he'd put his arms round her, this move of his she liked.

Mary stopped suddenly, pointed at the view across the lake and said. 'Isn't that a lovely scene Timothy?'

While she was talking he was looking at her red hair hanging down around her shoulders, her slim figure and her soft slender body. He thought how he'd like to hold her close and feel the softness of her against him. Yes, he'd have to get to know her better. While he was thinking these things about her, little did he realise, Mary was wondering what does he think of me, does he like me? Would he like, to take me out she wondered?

She gave the ball another kick, they ran after it and ended up trying to hold each other away from it.

It was time to start back. They did not realise they had walked so far, so they stopped where the two boats were moored. Mary sat into one and behaved as though she was the captain of a pirate ship. She walked up and down as the boat rocked in the water, thinking how she'd like to go out on the lake sometime.

To her surprise he said, 'would you like to go for a row now?'

'It's getting late and cold, perhaps another time,' she said.

The Bluebell's Mystery

'Right then, I'll tell you what, we'll meet some evening and I'll take you out fishing for a while. I might even catch a fish if I can get the loan of a fishing rod.'
The castle walls loomed high and grey as she headed for the servant's entrance. He went around to the front door. Mary felt happy she had a date to go boating.

When she arrived up to her room she was surprised to find Teresa sitting on the bed with tears in her eyes, she tried to hide her sadness.
'What's wrong, are you in some kind of trouble Teresa? Sit here and tell me.' Mary held her hand.
'Come on, tell me what's wrong.'
'I was thinking of my sister Ann who was a year younger than me. It was Christmas time and there had been a lot of heavy rain. Down at the back of our house there was a pond at the bottom of the field. It turned very cold and the pond froze over. Ann wandered out on to the ice. It was two hours before we found her body. I was thinking of her and of you, and how I have come to look on you as the sister I miss so much.'
Mary had her arms around Teresa and they both sat on the side of the bed crying.
'I'd be delighted if you would consider me a sister Teresa, but not to replace your sister Ann.'
Thinking of the tragedy was breaking Mary's heart.
After a while they headed down to the kitchen, where the conversation eventually came back to the state of their romantic lives.
'What did you think of the ceili last Friday?' asked Mary.
'You know, I had a great night and you'll never guess who I went out with.'
'Who was it, do I know him?'
'Yes you do, it was Sean Derey. You've seen him at the ceilies. He asked me out before. I'll go with him again, although it took me all my time just to keep him at bay. What happened with you and Timothy?'

'We've just been out for a walk. We had a good night at the ceili.'

'Sean and I were saying to each other that we might as well be on the moon. You didn't even know we were there! I was talking to Sandra and she told me she's related to Timothy, a cousin or something. It's funny us thinking she was his girlfriend.'

'Well don't forget Teresa that they did arrive together and they were with each other at the ball.'

'She knew you had your eye on him and she said that she could have played the part of a real witch,' we had a great laugh.

The days passed quickly and Mary and Timothy went for long walks. They spent as much time together as they could.

'I'm an Irish girl Timothy courting an Englishman in Ireland, what will my brother say when he hears about us? He didn't want me to come here to work in the first place, because he's anti anything to do with the English. For him to find out that I went out with you would drive him mad.'

'It will be all right Mary, very soon I'll be gone back to school.'

As he spoke to her he was thinking of how he felt. He wanted to hold her close and kiss her, tell her he loved her. They had a good time together, walking the secret pathways through the woods as they followed the stream. The gentle caress, looking at the pheasant as it went on its way, unaware it was being watched.

'I'm going to miss you when you go back to England Timothy.'

'It won't be long I'll be back here at Christmas. You won't find the time pass. Next time I'll be home for a longer stay, until then I'll go back and finish my schooling forever.'

They walked along the quiet places deep in their own sad thoughts, aware that they soon were parting for

The Bluebell's Mystery

what was only a short time but to them, seemed so long.

The castle came into view too soon. Timothy had to leave early in the morning. They kissed and he held her close while she shed a tear. Asking her not to cry seemed to make things even worse they reluctantly parted.

When she entered her bedroom Teresa noticed she'd been crying.

'Well I must say that if you're crying because he's leaving, things must be getting serious. You see when tears fall, it's time to watch out. You should be more like me Mary. When I part company with my fellows I always feel good. Anyway he'll be back in a few months and you won't find the time pass.'

As she lay in her bed she thought of how she felt about him. She wondered was she crazy, the masked ball, the boats, the ceili and the dancing. The shaking woke her.

'Come on let's go,' said Teresa. Things carried on the same as ever, Mary thought.

Chapter 23

'Cathleen's wedding is the next big occasion in our house Teresa.'
'Am I invited Mary?'
'You'll be invited alright,' she said as they started laughing. Mary's weekend off came around quickly. On her way home she thought of the things herself and Timothy enjoyed. Lately he seemed to be the only person on her mind. She was thinking how wrong everything was. His parents were of the British Imperialist landlord class. As soon as word got out at home and around the countryside, it would bring a great shame on the family. All this just because she liked him. None of these issues were important to her, her thoughts brought her tears and sadness. She wondered had she made a mistake. She should try and forget about him she thought. She made up her mind not see him again.

She noticed the sky with its mountainous white clouds. It was a nice day, the noise from the crows with their never ending squawks, the small birds chasing each other and the cheerful chirping of the sparrows, in the hedges. Some birds were like humans, they'd meet, fall in love have young and never part. They do not care which is Protestant or Catholic.

At the top of the hill she paused and looked down into the valley. Home was a long way off in a little quiet flat green patch, a white thatched stone house with a shed a little way to the right. To Mary this was a sanctuary. She felt safe there. So far thanks be to god even the British had not defiled this house.

'Hello Mary, I saw you coming across the hill, so I decided to come to meet you.' She could see the delight on her mother's face as they hugged each other. She could also see that age was beginning to show in her mother's body. Her stride had slowed and her youthful energy had eased. They sat and talked beside the fire, Mary watched the flickering flame, which allowed her mind to wander. Her mother walked towards the door and said. 'I'm going out to see if I can find that hen's nest. She's a nuisance.'

The warmth of the fire, the comfort and relaxation of being at home, the yellow and pinkish colouring of the flame, the soothing smell of the burning turf, brought pleasant feelings to Mary's mind. This peaceful and comfortable state and the hypnotic glowing flame had Mary asleep before her mother arrived back.

Rose O'Shea sat down by the fire and let its magic take her on a trip back to the past, way beyond Famine times to when she was young and as good looking as her daughter. She remembered the bad and the good times. She thanked god that she and her family had made it through the Famine and wondered what road life was going to take her family down. There was a lot of talk about America. To go there was costly, although land was cheap she'd heard. When Mary wakes from her sleep they'd have a chat about all these things.

Mary woke to a busy house. Peter's 'Hello, did you have a good sleep?' brought laughter from Tom and Cathleen.

There was a pleasant atmosphere and the worries, woes and wants of the times they lived in didn't take from the good feelings of home. After a while she was telling Cathleen and her mother about the masked ball and the dresses she and Teresa had made. How Mrs. Melen got two of the ladies to wear them and what happened after that.

Smiling Cathleen asked, 'who did she get to wear them?'

'You'll never guess.'

'Come on, tell us.'

'Teresa and myself.'

Cathleen clapped her hands, "Ho-Ho" how did you feel?'
'We were afraid, we were terrified Cathleen. Here we were mixing with the gentry and the elegant ladies. They couldn't know who we were with our masks on, but I must say our dresses did make a good impression!'
'Did you by any chance dance with any handsome Englishmen?' Cathleen and her mother started laughing.
Mary didn't mention anything about Timothy.
Peter interrupted with the remark. 'I heard you and Teresa were talking to some English fellow and his girlfriend at the ceili.'
'He is the youngest son of the Melens, he goes to school in England. He was here on holidays and he brought that girl over for the celebrations.'
'I heard he gave you a few dances that night. I hope you're not getting involved with an Englishman-believe you me that's the last thing we want to see happening.'
'Don't you start that row again Peter. Anyway I'll go out with who ever I like. You learn to mind your own business about my private life.'
'Why are you getting upset Mary if it's of no consequence?'
'You're trying to start that old row again aren't you? Anyway did any of your pals meet his girlfriend?'
"Oh yes, I was told she's good looking.'
'If you had been to the ceili you would have tried to go with her. That would really have got things going wouldn't it?' she shouted.
'If I had been there and tried to ask her out, that would have been a right surprise to her boyfriend.'
'So it would have been alright for you Peter to ask her but not so for me?'
This made him think a little.
'Timothy liked the ceili, he gave me a few dances, don't make a big deal out of it.'

The Bluebell's Mystery

Cathleen, standing up, held her arms out as if to dance, and said. 'Like this?' It took the nastiness out of the conversation.

'What did you think of the style of the ladies at the ball Mary?' Cathleen asked as she waltzed Mary around the kitchen floor.

Mary whispered. 'Some of the dresses were low cut and very revealing. If the priest had seen the way they were dressed, he'd have had them excommunicated. Her brothers, not having heard this, were stunned by the laughter.

'What about the dresses you and Teresa made?' Did they really make an impression on the ladies?'

'Oh yes and on the men as well because we were danced all night.'

'Well then when are we going to see them.'

'You won't get to see them now Cathleen, I'm afraid they're gone to England.'

'What do you mean I'd like to have seen them.'

'I'll bring you home the sketches that we made before Marion Shelten took them away. She's a friend of the Melens, and she offered us jobs in London and gave us the fare to persuade us to go. So you see Peter, I've nearly enough money to get you to America. When you do go, I think I might go with you, alright?'

'Yes Mary that is a good idea we might go together yet.'

Mary asked Cathleen. 'When is your wedding going to take place?'

'We've decided to postpone it for a while. Do you remember we spoke about a man who helps people to get to America and he gets them land? Well we're looking into that.'

"But what about the wedding?'

'We'll get married before we leave. As you know, things are not good here.'

'If things keep going the way they are there won't be anyone left in the country,' said her father.

After a night's sleep Mary was buzzing around getting the dinner and making bread, while her mother and father were outside working in the garden.

'Mary, you seemed to get into a bit of a state last night when we were talking about that young Melen fellow.'

'Don't tell anyone Cathleen, but the fact is that Timothy and I went out a few times.' She saw a frown on Cathleen's face.

'Don't worry, I'm not going to get involved. He's gone back to England anyway. Have your wedding here and we'll invite everybody. Jokingly she said, 'what if Timothy is back from England, can I invite him?'

'I thought you weren't interested in him anymore and now you want to invite him to my wedding?'

Mary blushed saying, 'But I was only joking.'

'Surely he would be too grand for one of our weddings Mary.'

'Who cares and I'll tell you what, if Sandra comes home with him we'll invite her as well.'

Cathleen replied saying: 'Alright and if the queen likes she can come too.' Both of them had a good laugh.

'You should invite a few of the girls you knew at school, the boys would have a great time.'

'What will we give them to eat?'

'We'll give them a good time, just let them enjoy themselves, and make your wedding a farewell party.'

Chapter 24

Having arrived back in England tired from travelling Timothy was amazed that all he seemed to think about was Mary O'Shea. Why should I be thinking of her? What am I doing? I could get myself killed for going out with an Irish colleen. He smiled. Sandra said she enjoyed the ceili so much that she'd go back with him the next time he was going home. She must have thrown her eye on some Irish fellow, what a laugh! Right now he'd get down to his studies and forget all about Mary. He thought of a plan to get her out of his mind. It was working well he thought as he went to sleep thinking of her and the plan.

The weeks were passing quickly. Mary was back home for a few days. Working in the kitchen her attention was caught by her brother Tom.
'You're very quiet Tom, what are you doing with yourself these times?'
'I'm working for John Curtis. I saw you at the ceili with that English lad and two girls but I couldn't stay that night. Was one of their names Boyle?'
'Yes I work with Teresa, do you know her.'
'I saw her at ceilies before.'
'Would you like me to introduce you to her sometime?' This caused a laugh.
'What about the other girl, is she English?'
"Yes she is, she was here for the celebrations at Melen's. Sandra is her name. If she ever comes back I'll introduce you to her.'
'If she has any common sense she won't come back here. Are you happy working in Melen's?'
'Yes it's a big place, it's hard work but its fine.'
To make a joke Tom said. 'If Sandra ever comes back again introduce me to her. I'm sure she'll love to meet

an Irishman, especially one with red hair like mine.' He pulled his hand through his hair and tossed it.

'She's quite a pleasant girl Tom, a lot of the fellas at the ceili fancied her, it's a pity you didn't stay.'

'Maybe that's the way it's to be.'

'Cathleen you and Jim should go to the ceili the odd time. You'd meet some of your old friends.'

'Tell me about this Timothy fellow, when will he be back here again?'

'Now listen Cathleen, I'm trying to get him out of my mind and avoiding anything to do with him and here you are asking me when he will be back. As far as I know he'll be here around Christmas and then he goes back to college to do his finals.'

Next morning Mary felt sad leaving the house. She'd enjoyed being at home with Cathleen and her brothers. Looking at the trees she could see the changes. Autumn was setting in, the colours were breathtaking, an artist's delight. The colours could not be described only absorbed and delighted in they were beautiful. The birds quivered and swayed and zipped past in their usual hurry. She didn't mind going to work this lovely morning. The fact that Timothy wasn't going to be there brought sadness. As they prepared the dinner Teresa said. 'What did you think of the offer of a job we got from Mrs. Shelten?'

'To be honest with you Teresa I'm still in shock, everything happened so quickly. I consider it the chance of a lifetime and when Timothy comes home at Christmas I'd advise you to go back with him and take the job.'

'I'm sorry I didn't go over with him this time and if I didn't like it I could have come back here. That would have been smart wouldn't it Mary?'

'Cathleen told me she is going to America with Jim, but she'll definitely get married before she goes. You are invited and so is anyone else I would like to bring.'

'You never know the way things work out Mary. Timothy might be back here before the wedding.'
'Do you think it would be alright to bring him Teresa?'
'Yes if he's here in time.'
'That would be good,' said Mary laughing.

All the talking left them tired and the kitchen spotless.
'Did you ever meet my brothers Tom and Peter?'
'No, they haven't been that lucky, why?'
'It seems Tom saw you and Sandra at the ceili and according to him you two are mighty good looking girls.'
'You tell Tom he flatters us.'

'If you are thinking of going to England Teresa you should make a special dress or coat to take with you to Marion Shelten.'
'That's a good idea Mary. If we make two more special designs you can take one with you to America. You might even go into the fashion business over there.'
'Isn't it amazing the way things have changed since the ball? Already we are talking about designing for the fashion industry. We've a lot to do Teresa.'

Chapter 25

Having caught up with Peter and the cattle on the Mortha road Tom heard the sound of a whistle. This signal told him the police were up ahead with his father. He quickly drove the cattle through the ditch as planned. One of them went into the field and the contrary one was left on the road. The sound of the whistle also warned Peter and the Henderson lad to leave and head for home across the fields. They stayed close to the ditches to avoid being seen. Three policemen came around the bend and stopped in front of Tom.

'Did you see any cattle when you were coming along this road?' Shouted one of the policemen.

'Yes I did back there around the bend. I nearly broke my neck when I walked into a bullock.'

'There were cattle stolen from one of the estates. It's strange that you and your father are on this particular road at the same time isn't it? What the hell are you doing out here at this time of night anyway?'

'I came over to see Katie Martin, she lives down the road.'

The police then decided to go back and see did James have a whistle on him.

'Empty your pockets,' one of them shouted at him.

'What the hell is this about?'

'Just empty out your pockets and do it now,' he was told. 'Where are you coming from at this hour?'

'I was over in Ollie O'Neill's playing cards. I was lucky see, I won a shilling.'

'Did you blow a whistle?'

'Ah, so that's what the noise was? It sounded funny. I heard it alright.'

The Bluebell's Mystery

'I met your son back there and it seems there's a stolen bullock on the road close to him, it's all a bit of a coincidence, isn't it?'
'Ah sure the whole world is a bit of a coincidence when you think about it. He comes over here sometimes to see a Miss Martin. If you're going back that way now, tell him to hurry and I'll wait a few minutes for him.'
'We'll check out your answers and if there's anything strange we'll be back to you.'
The O'Neill's and the Martin's had already been warned about the evening's events.

Chapter 26

Mary introduced her brothers to Teresa at the ceili a few weeks later.
'I think your brothers are a little shy with girls Mary.'
'I didn't know that but most fellows are. Maybe it's because they were talking to such an attractive girl.'
Teresa began to laugh.
Mary's old boyfriend was there and he was drunk as usual, but she didn't bother with him. One of the lads working at the castle got the privilege of driving them back to their workplace. Tom headed home with his girlfriend. Peter stayed on with his friends and they had a good few drinks, and as usual they got rowdy and anti-British. On their way home they decided to attack the barracks. There was a gang of about six lads. They started throwing stones at the barracks and when the police came running outside some of them were hit.
'Oh- oh,' shouted one man as he fell down holding his head. Some of the lads went round to the back of the barracks while the peelers were out the front, they set the place on fire. One of the police recognised Peter, even though he had his face half covered.
'You're Peter O'Shea aren't you?' he shouted loudly.
Peter pulled back startled, because he knew he was in trouble.
'Damn this poteen,' he muttered as he distanced himself from the place.
When he looked back at the barracks it was burning fiercely. There were policemen on horses shouting loudly. Peter knew he'd better not go home tonight. Things had changed for the worst so he headed for a hideaway that he and Tom had built years ago. He would be warm and out of the way there. Tom would know where to find him.

'What the hell happened after I left the ceili, Peter?' Tom said in an angry way.
'On the way home a few pals and myself decided to burn the barracks.'
'Do you remember what happened to John Curtis's son?'
'Yes don't you know I do, why do you think I'm hiding here?'
'By God now you're in trouble, you know you're going to have to stay in hiding for a while, because they'll be watching everything. I'll check to see if we can get you to America.

Tom went towards home and met his father at the front of the house and asked him.
'Did you hear about Peter yet?'
'No, what in heaven's name has happened to him now?'
'He and a few of his pals were spotted burning the barracks.'
'Again,' said his father. 'That was a daft idea, be sure not to tell your mother, she hasn't been feeling well for a while.'
'Cathleen's fellow will know something soon about America.'
The next morning the police called to the house and shouted at Mrs. O'Shea. 'Where is that good-for-nothing son of yours?'
'Which of my sons are you talking about?'
'Peter,' shouted the guard. 'He'll go to jail for this.'
'What did he do?' she asked.
'He burned the barracks last night and one of our men was hurt.'
Rose began to cry uncontrollably. Mary put her arms around her and helped her back into the kitchen.
When James arrived home he cursed the police for their ignorance. He couldn't get Rose to stop crying. The police called a few more times looking for Peter, and each time they behaved badly towards the O'Sheas.

'Is there any chance of getting Peter out of this country quickly Tom?'
'We'll need money to do that Mary.'
'I have some,' she took it from her pocket.
'Where did you get all that?'
'We got well paid for the dresses we made.'
'You sure did, with that much we have enough. Your dressmaking must have created a good impression. What will you do now Mary?'
'I told Peter if I made money I'd help him get to America and then he could send for me.'
'Do you think you'll go?'
'Right now I don't know anything.' She felt she had just given away her only chance of ever getting there. She went to bed and cried herself to sleep thinking of Peter and Timothy. Would she ever, see him again? If he heard this story about her brother would he bother about her? She decided that nobody could take her dreams away from her not even Timothy, so she could sleep with him in her dreams and leave this mess behind.

All too soon it was time to go back to work. She thought that while things kept changing in her life and it became unpredictable, the countryside, although it changed annually had a more constant way about it. Mary arrived into work tired and confused and sick of everything.

Time passed slowly and Mary's impatience did not help her one bit. It would be another three weeks or so before Timothy arrived. She'd probably be at the wedding that weekend, because she'd have a few days off.

Mary laughed at the behaviour of Teresa when she came into their room one evening and started to speak in a low whisper.
'I found out something Mary. It's something you are going to want to know about.' She danced around the floor keeping her secret.

Mary began guessing; 'Your boyfriend asked you to marry him?' At this they started laughing. You were asked to go to America by your great-grand uncle?'
'Wrong again,' shouted Teresa.
'Come on then, tell me,' said Mary smiling.
'All right, all right. Martin the stable hand told Mrs. Ward that the young Melen lad and his cousin arrived today.'
'Are you serious? I'm amazed Sandra came back with him. She must have liked being here the last time.'
Mary couldn't care less, all she could think of was Timothy. She felt shocked and delighted but she didn't let Teresa notice this.
'I'll tell you what we'll do Teresa, we'll go down to the kitchen, have a mug of tea, steal two of those lovely cakes Mrs. Ward's forever trying to hide and we'll celebrate.'
'You know something Mary there are times when I think you're quite intelligent.'

Chapter 27

It didn't take long for Timothy to find Mary. Soon they were walking the secret places of this huge estate. The hideaways where young lovers enjoy their secret meetings, the places they think no one else in the world knows about. Here he'd hold her close and feel the softness of her body. She asked him an obvious question.
 'Did you miss me when you were away?'
'Well to tell the truth I did feel a little bit lonely leaving home but once I got to England I forgot all about Ireland.'
He let her think he had no thoughts about her.
She knew by his jolly behaviour that he was telling her white lies, so she decided to play him at his own game.
'You know you are not supposed to be back here for another three weeks or so.'
'Will my being here,' he said in a serious tone, 'interfere with your social life Mary?'
'Of course it will,' she teased him. 'It will make it great.'
'We're allowed a month or so off but we are still supposed to keep up our studies. There's a bit of renovating happening at the college. I have only one more term to do.'
'What do you think you'll do then?'
'I was considering going to America or I can stay in England. Some of the chaps at college asked me to go to America with them. You know I might even come back here and marry you.' At this they started laughing. She started to run, he chased her and he kissed her.
'There's just one thing you forgot in your great assessment of the situation...I might not necessarily want to marry you.'

The Bluebell's Mystery

He held her close and they kissed, walked and talked.
When Mary arrived back to the kitchen Teresa was quick to remark. 'It didn't take you long to get together. Why did he take Sandra back with him?'
'It seems she wanted to come.'
'At least I'll have someone to take to the ceilies. She does attract men. If I stick close to her I'll be surrounded by lots of them, even though she is English.'
They were standing laughing when Helen Melen came round the corner and caught them and this made them laugh more.
'What are you two laughing at?'
'I think we've just got the giggles.'
She went away smiling.
'Mary, remember I said that I was going to take the job with the fashion woman? Well I'm going to go back with Timothy and Sandra this time.'
'If you go and you don't like it Teresa, you will be able to come back and the two of us might go to America together.'
'Mary why do you always talk about America?'
'Because I couldn't see any of my brothers going to England, considering how much they dislike the British. If they are in America I will have someone to go to.'
'There's a ceili soon, will you go with Timothy and Sandra?'
'I will but there is just one thing, the eye will be on Timothy because he's English. The fellows don't mind Sandra because she's a girl. Typical men, they are really stupid, they'll try and play with her. If it's an Englishman they'll try and kill him.
'In a way we can't really blame them for that, don't forget the English are to blame for most of our troubles but I have an idea, and it's good.'
"You surprise me Teresa, a good idea coming from you. What is it? Tell me quickly before you forget.' Teresa

could see the change in Mary's attitude to everything. She was a much happier person since Timothy arrived.
'Firstly, there's no need for that smartness.' Now the laughing really got going.
'You go to the ceili with your brothers, I'll arrive with Sandra and Timothy, and everybody will think he is with me. Your brothers will dance with Sandra and me.' Timothy will dance with you.'
'That's not a bad idea Teresa, it might work.'
   'The police are after Peter you know. He got involved with some fellows who decided to burn the barracks again. Now he has to keep a low profile. I think the only safe place for him is America. There's always some problem isn't there Teresa?'
A week later they went to the ceili, and they pulled it off as Teresa had said. Tom danced with Sandra and Teresa. Timothy and Mary danced with different partners so as not to make it obvious they were together.
'Hello Sandra, how are you doing,' said Tom.
She was taken back a little and replied. 'How do you know my name,' she said in her English accent.
He started laughing. 'Do you know Mary O'Shea?'
'Yes I do.'
'Well she's my sister.'
'Oh I see, I should have known that. I was told one of her brothers had red hair. Mary told me things about you, that you're a wild man.' They started to laugh, and he noticed her good looks.
'You must not believe anything Mary says about me. You look attractive tonight.'
'Thank you very much,' she blushed.
'Do you like Ireland?'
'Yes the people are nice.'
'Are you going to stay long?'
'I'm going to stay until my cousin Timothy goes back to college.'
'Timothy who?'

The Bluebell's Mystery

'Timothy Melen.'

'So that is who he is, I take it he and Mary are seeing each other.'

'I would say so,' she replied, 'is there anything wrong with that?'

'I suppose not, except that my sister was keeping it a secret from us.'

They danced around as if they had been dancing together all their lives. When he danced with Teresa he enjoyed himself, yet when he was with Sandra they got on great. It should not be like this. She's English. What, the hell about it? She's good looking. He decided he'd try to ask her out.

'Sandra, as you will not be going back to England for a few weeks why don't we meet some evening, we could go for a walk.'

She surprised him when she said: 'I don't mind going for a walk with you.'

'Don't tell Timothy or Mary and I'll meet you at the entrance gates to Melen's on Wednesday evening, say eight o'clock.'

'Okay, I'll see you then.'

Tom was surprised.

There was a lull in the dancing and Mary saw Peter talking to some fellows behind the band.

'Mary I think this might be the last time I'll get to a ceili before I go away. That's the reason I'm here tonight. I'm going to enjoy myself as best I can.'

'What in heavens name are you thinking about at all, you know that if they catch you they'll put you in jail,' she said almost crying.

'It will be alright Mary, I'll get to America, don't you worry.'

'You should be over there now. Don't get caught here, go soon.'

'Thanks for the money Mary, I'll let you know everything when I get there and I'll send for you. Now

I'm going to dance with your two friends, is that all right?'
Mary cried as he gave her a goodbye kiss on the cheek. Peter stood in front of Sandra and he introduced himself and asked her to dance. She glanced at Mary and noticed the tears. She looked at Peter and asked in her strange accent, 'is Mary alright?'
'Yes she's grand.'
They danced and he enjoyed her company, he noticed her good looks and hoped that some day he might meet a girl like her and marry.
Peter then asked Teresa Boyle to dance.
'You're Mary's brother aren't you? I've seen you at ceilies before.'
'If I had asked you out would you have gone out with me?'
In the middle of the laughing she said: 'Well if you had asked me out then I might have.'
'You know something you are cute.'
He heard the sound of the whistle, stood back a step, gave Teresa a kiss on the cheek and said: 'That's my call, I must go.'
By the time the police started asking questions, Peter and his friends were gone.
Timothy and Sandra were shocked by the antics of the police.
'What are you two doing at this ceili? Do you realise you're in dangerous company, considering you're English?'
'We've been to these ceili's before and we never had any trouble. We've always enjoyed ourselves.'
'Well you better watch out because I think you're in the wrong company.'
The police didn't realise that whoever was in the company of the O'Shea's was safe.
The musicians decided they were not going to let the police officers destroy the night. They made sure that everybody enjoyed the dance to the end. Going to sleep

The Bluebell's Mystery

Mary's thoughts were on Peter and his problems. She wondered had Sandra and Timothy heard anything about her brother. If and when Timothy did, would he be upset at the O'Shea's?

The girls were talking as they made the breakfast and prepared the dinner at Melen's.
'Mary, Sandra said she enjoyed herself great at the ceili, and Tom seemed to take her fancy or was it Peter? Any news of the wedding?'
'They're getting married before they head to America with a man who has organised land for those who want to buy it.'
They're lucky she thought, and wondered would things work out for her. She'd wait and see how she and Timothy got on together in the next few months. She dreamt of marrying him some day and going to the New World. It's only a dream she thought. Her wishful thinking made her sad. They were meeting more often and walking round the woods made them familiar with all the secret places.

Their behaviour was noticed by the Melen family, this caused them to be concerned. One evening while having tea together, his mother said to him. 'Timothy I see that you and Mary O'Shea are meeting quite often. Do you know what you are doing? Don't you know it's not right for you to have anything to do with this girl?'
'Don't worry about it mother, we're only having a bit of a time together. In a short while I'll go back to school and it will all be forgotten.'
'It's not wise to do this Timothy, you being the son of an English landlord and she an Irish peasant girl. Don't lead her on and then go back to school and forget about her that would be terrible. Do you know what happens to an Irish girl, who carries on with an Englishman? She becomes the talk of the country...her family are talked about and the Church she belongs to, disowns her. Make sure that you don't make her a

disgrace to her family and her friends, do you hear me?'
'Mother, Mary and myself get on well together.'
'I don't care how you get on, you look after her.'
'Okay mother I'll do as you say.'
After his conversation with his mother and her concern for Mary, Timothy decided they would keep their meetings secret. In their romancing with each other, they soon realised they were falling in love. Their feelings were so strong it was frightening and wonderful. They both were in a world of their own. Their feelings for each other made them take liberties. It was a wonderful passionate time that they enjoyed. They laughed, hugged and kissed, and it was a reality to be relived in thought, again and again.

Chapter 28

On the way home from the ceili discussing Peter's problems, Tom said. 'We'll try and get you out on the same ship as Cathleen and Jim if they ever get married.'
'Don't you know that's the very ship the British will be watching Tom?'
'It will be dangerous but we have to get you out.'
'We were lucky we had someone standing guard at the ceili tonight Tom. It was a pity the police arrived and spoiled everything, it was one of the best dances I was at in a long time.'
 'What did you think of the English girl? She's good looking, I wouldn't mind going out with her.'
'You had your chance, so why didn't you ask her out Tom.'
'Things were not just right. If I meet her again I'll have a go.' He didn't tell Peter he'd already asked her out.
'It's a pity I have to leave Tom. I danced with Mary's friend from work, she's nicely built. I've seen her at ceilies before, but I didn't have the nerve to ask her out.'
"Would you have liked to?'
'Oh, yes!' Peter answered.
'You know you probably won't see her again?'
"I would have the courage to ask her out now that I'm going away.'
'That's the trouble, we all have the courage when it's too late.'
'A question Tom, what is going on with you and father and the poteen?'
'It's going all right, but I don't think I'm going to stay here stealing cattle and making poteen for the rest of my life.'

'Wouldn't it be grand to be heading out either to America or God forbid to England with one of those girls we spoke to tonight?'
Tom was so happy he couldn't keep his secret any longer.
'Do you know Peter, I took a terrible chance at the ceili but it was worth it.'
'What did you do?'
'I asked Sandra to meet me next week and she said yes. I'm not waiting around any longer for things to happen, because we're the ones who have to make them happen.'
Peter was thinking he'd move on Teresa the next time he'd see her if, he ever saw her again.
'What do you think of that Melen chap going out with our sister Tom?'
'Well I think Mary is able to look after herself, there are things women know that we men don't and one of them is how to take care of themselves.'
'I hope so because he is British and they have no respect for the Irish.'
'The trouble with women is, they won't let anyone get close to them.' Tom pulled his coat around him to keep the cold away.

   There were two or three potato cakes and some bread on the table when they arrived home so they had a hunger-satisfying meal. They were getting into bed when they should have been getting out, they knew things were changing fast.
When they arrived into the kitchen for breakfast, their father asked them.
'How did things go at the ceile last night?'
'Peter was with the O'Neill boys. They had a man watching for the police and as soon as they came near the ceili we left quietly.'
'I hope to god they don't come here harassing us again.'
'Peter and I were talking about America last night.'
James turned and surprised him by saying.

'I think that's a good idea. The two of you should go together and that way you'll look out for each other. Why don't you get smart boys, go and see the man Cathleen spoke about, perhaps he can get you land over there.' James knew there was nothing here for young men only trouble and that they'd be better off in a land where they'd be free.

That evening James and Rose sat on an old log outside drinking a cup of poteen each - for Rose O'Shea a terrible sin, even though her husband made it. They talked of the old days when they fought through the Famine years against hunger and disease. How they struggled to raise the family against all the odds and now just when things seem to be coming right, there's emigration in the wind.

'Don't worry Rose,' James said in a sad tone. So long as we have enough of the crator to see you, me and old Curtis out, we'll wish them all well, God bless and good luck.'

They held hands and cried their way back to the house. Each wrapped in their thoughts of days gone by when they were as young as their sons and daughters are now... the days when they were courting. When the English had the country by the throat as indeed they still had. They knew things were changing fast. At least they'd see, Cathleen married and that alone was a blessing. Rose worried about Mary. Maybe she'll get herself a husband. Living on her own life could be tough so she'd ask God to look after her.

Chapter 29

'Cathleen and Jim are going to America when they are married Teresa.'
'Why don't you go with them?'
'I'm going to wait until they're out there and then I'll consider going.'
'I'm definitely going to England this time.'
'I'm glad for you Teresa and I hope you do well in the fashion industry. If I run into any problems in life I'll always be able to go and join you.'
'Yes, that would be great, we could experiment with new styles again.'
'We did all right with those dresses,' Mary said smiling.
'We must have raised an eyebrow or two.'
'Are you going to stay here in Melen's?'
'I'm not too sure about that yet.'
There were changes taking place in Mary's body that she didn't want anyone to know about just yet. It was telling her that she and Timothy had let their love for each other cross the line of no return and right now all she could do was find quiet places to cry. Perhaps it's only a severe 'flu or a cold, so she asked God to let it be so. He was the only one she could turn to. Should she tell Timothy, she knew he loved her? At least she thought he did. It might spoil the finishing of his schooling so she decided against that. Tell her mother? Not now, she'd find out soon enough. Should she tell Teresa, no she might tell Timothy and that would make a mess of things, so she decided not to tell anyone. She wondered how Timothy would feel when he heard the news about her.
Thinking of her situation when alone made her cry her heart out. To become pregnant outside of marriage in Ireland at this time was frowned on. It would bring

disgrace to the family. When Timothy heard this, would he come back from England for her or would he just go on the boat and head to America?

She wiped her tears and then she cried a little more. She'd wait until they were all gone, and then she'd go home and have her baby and hope her mother would not be upset.

When would she start to show signs she was pregnant? She'd be able to make herself bigger clothes, although people were not always that easily fooled. She thought of how things can change and on this change depends, her whole life.

She imagined herself at home with her mother and father. She had spent her years caring for her parents, as her child grew older. She had never married. She pictured herself, a young woman walking towards the river with a boy of eleven. He was running around throwing stones and chasing the birds. She looked at the woman and could see a lonely sadness about her. Years of living on her own and raising her child, the disappointment of being abandoned by the man she loved had taken its toll. She knew these were just her own imaginary feelings haunting her.

Was this what the situation was going to be for her, her tears fell easily now. The happiness of having a little boy or girl, the sadness of missing out on what might have been... like going to America or England, exploring the fashion industry, making it her own playground, being the maker of the best and most beautiful styles. Working to reach the top, and enjoying the effort, being married to Timothy and having a wonderful fulfilling life and the children she so wished for. Was all that gone now due to this one moment of happiness she and Timothy had had? Was it going to destroy her life and his? If he only knew how much she loved him. Oh! Timothy it's a crazy mess! Would she have to stay in this troubled land and raise her child on her own? She would always be wondering if Timothy went to America on his own, or did he meet someone else? Her thoughts at this time turned to god. She said a prayer, and asked Him to forgive her for her mistake. After her minds little sojourn into the past and the future, she got hold of herself before Teresa or anybody else came. As she went about her chores she consoled herself with the fact that nobody knew yet. She'd behave as though there was nothing wrong, get up early, go for a walk and hide herself in the mornings.

True to form, Tom met Sandra at the castle gates it was almost dark. She wore a long brown coat, over a bright red dress. Her fair hair hung down to her shoulders, her complexion was pale and she looked nice.
'Have you been waiting long Tom?'
'No just a short while.' He held her by the hand and was surprised to find she was at ease with that.
He faced her, held her other hand and said: 'I think you're lovely.'
He could see a glint in her blue eyes and he knew by her smile, she was happy to see him. He leaned in close to kiss her, she turned and he kissed her cheek. Laughing he said, 'you got me that time.' She blushed and they walked on.
'What did you think of the ceili the other night?'
She smiled and replied saying, 'It was one of the best nights I've had in a long time. You Irish are a great and peculiar people.'
'Why so Sandra?'
'Here you are in a troubled country and you just go out and enjoy yourselves, the music and the dancing was great?'
She liked the way his curly red hair was combed back. She saw his solid stature and his strong stride as they walked side by side.
'The girls told me you might be going to America Tom.'
'Yes I think it might be the best thing to do. I also like the idea of a new world. It must be something to arrive

on those shores and realise that it's up to one's self to either win or lose. I'll tell you what,' he said smiling. 'Would you like to come with me? It would be a great adventure.'
'Would it surprise you to know that lots of English people go to America? It has been discussed at home by some of my brothers. I have considered going myself,' she said.
The conversation was lively. He put his arm around her, she allowed this as she guided him back towards the castle gates. They stood against the pier and he kissed her. They stayed for quite a while.
'Sandra, when are you going to go back to England?'
'It's funny you should ask me that,' she smiled.
'Why?'
'Well don't forget only a little while ago you asked me to go to America with you. Were you serious?'
'Of course I was.' She had put him in a corner and he didn't know whether he was coming or going.
'When I go back home I'll ask my brothers to make up their minds and if they are not going, I'm going on my own.'
'Well I'll put it this way Sandra, you can bother with your brothers if you like, but I'll tell you this. I'll go over to England with you and we'll discuss the situation with them and either way you and I will go. How is that for a suggestion?'
She surprised Tom when she answered him saying: 'Do you want to bother staying here until Timothy is going back to school?'
'Not really. You and I could be well in America by then,' he said.
'But you're a total stranger to me Tom.'
'I know that but I like you and if I see you a few more times we'll be good friends.' They held each other close while he kissed her.
'I'll see you again here on Thursday.'
He kissed her again before they parted.

The Bluebell's Mystery

Tom went away wondering was he crazy, what exactly had they been talking about? He could not understand how all this happened, but he was delighted. She seemed eager to get to America. He decided to wait a while before he'd tell anyone. He walked along with a skip in his step. He thought about his father. He'd be happy. Hadn't he often said, it was not right for young men to have to steal cattle and risk having to go to jail. The thought of the sailing, and the adventure made him feel anxious.

Sandra went back to the castle thinking, was she mad. The first time she'd seen him at the ceili she thought his red hair was most unusual. She liked its wild colour. He was courteous and good mannered and she liked him. After tonight she knew she'd venture to America with him rather than any of her brothers. He's handsome and Oh! God he's Irish. What will, my people think of him? She felt that it was someone like him she needed to take the anxieties out of going away, from her. He didn't seem to be worried, what she didn't know was that the years of stealing cattle and making poteen made him adventurous.

When Tom and Cathleen were having breakfast next morning he told her about Sandra. She was surprised. 'Why don't you go and see that man I told you about? He might be able to get you land in America.'

'That's a good idea I'll do that.'

A few days later Tom followed Cathleen's advice and went to see this man. He got a shock when he discovered he'd get approximately two hundred acres of land.

In his wisdom he asked. 'Is it possible that my brother Peter could get some?'

'Are you both married and are you bringing your wives?'

'We are bringing our girlfriends and we'll get married over there.'

He then remarked to Tom. 'Well at least you're young enough.'

'What has that got to do with anything?'

'Well to tell you the truth it's a young man's country out there, hard and tough.'

'It can't be any worse than here. If I don't get out of Ireland I'll end up in jail.'

'Oh then, I'll take you and your two ladies. Here, are the sailing dates, so get ready to sail.'

Tom related the story to his mother and father that evening, they were sad to think their sons were leaving but glad for them at the same time. He told Peter what the man said. 'I will take you and your two ladies.'

'But I don't have a girl.'

'I didn't have one until I made a date with Sandra,' said Tom, 'so why don't you talk to Teresa? Even if you did go to America you would not have to stay together.'

'You're right. If I'm lucky enough to meet her again I'll ask her.'

'Don't forget she might want to go but no one likes to start on a journey like that alone, especially a girl. Make sure you ask her.'

Chapter 30

The peacefulness of the O'Shea household was shattered once again with a loud bang on the door and the shout. 'This is the police, open up now or we'll break this door down. The house is surrounded. We want to question Peter O'Shea now!' shouted the sergeant.
James jumped from his bed and opened the door. He could feel the cold of the morning air blow into the house. He shouted at the police.
'What do you want him for?'
'You know well. He is being arrested for trying to burn the police barracks.'
Rose started crying, and the intimidating attitude of the police brought tension. Peter got ready to go out to them. One of the peelers got over - anxious and ventured into the house.
'Stop there,' shouted Tom stepping in front of him. The policeman moved to strike. James hit him on the head, and two more policemen rushed in. Sergeant Farrell roared. 'Hold it.' He saw Peter coming to the door.
He had decided to go quietly in order not to put the family through any more trouble.
'Your name is Peter O'Shea,' said the sergeant.
'And well you know it, we met before.'
'I'm arresting you for endeavouring to burn Her Majesty's Police Barracks.'
'Sadly enough we didn't succeed and it's a pity you were not inside', said Peter. The policemen marched him away.
Tom put his hands on his head shouting: 'Why didn't he get away from here sooner? God but we're stupid... what the hell do we do now? A week or two and he'd have been gone. We'll have to think of a plan to get him

out of jail and this time there will be no hanging around. What do the police do now?' he asked his father.

'They'll keep him here in the station for a couple of days, then move him to a more secure place. They'll try him for assault, sentence him and ship him out to Australia or some other place. Do you know that he could get as much as ten years for this.' said James.

'We'll work out a way of getting him out of jail father and this time it's straight to the boat. I remember you telling me something about this Sargeant Farrell. '

'John Curtis reckons it's possible that he could be related to the man who tried to burn the police station years ago, the time his son got caught.'

'We'll see to it that Peter is not shipped off to prison in Australia. Where does this Farrell man live? I'm going to see him and I'll find out everything about the Farrells.'

'He lives down the Mortha road where you supposedly go to see Miss Martin.'

Tom called at Farrell's house. It was a small cottage almost derelict at the end of a lane so overgrown that it looked like it was part of the ditch. It would be a good hiding place. Surely it's not possible for anyone to live here? He felt he was going cap in hand to see the very man he thought was only being smart at the market, but he must be on the inside.

He knocked on the door, wondering could he be lucky enough to find this man at home. The door opened. 'Ah! hello, so we meet again,' said Patrick Farrell smiling.

'You do remember me don't you? It was you and your Mr. McCoy who beat me up at the Curtis farm.'

'I have to do these things sometimes to keep Her Majesty on my side. I sometimes have to treat my own people badly as you well know.'

'I'm here to talk to you about my brother Peter.'

'Oh yes, the gobshite got caught.'

'I'll tell you what to do Tom. Why don't we have a meeting in Curtis's house tonight.'
Later that night having a drink, they thought out a plan that might work and they knew that this would be their last chance.

As the police marched Peter along to the barracks he was annoyed at himself for being so careless. He thought he'd have no trouble getting to America, but right now he felt stupid. If these bastards can keep me in jail they will leave me to rot. He remembered the great night he had at the ceili, Teresa, her looks and her figure held his mind for a while and took it away from the peelers. She looked nice with her black hair held in place with a white ribbon. Tom was right I should be on my way to America with the likes of her, not going to jail with this lot. It was time to forget about Teresa and figure a way out of this mess he thought.
Tom might get to see me and he might have some ideas of how to get me out of jail, I'll ask him to help. Soon he was being led through the village. The local people knew, he had been on the run and thought he was gone, but when they saw him being led along by the police they heckled.

Chapter 31

Teresa made her way home for the weekend. She had not been home for about four weeks. Her mind would not allow her to think of anything else but Mrs. Shelten. She was aware of the situation between Ireland and England but she could not do much about it. She'd tell her mother and father that if Mary O'Shea went with her, she'd go to London. Her mother surprised her saying: 'Listen Teresa you should go to London anyway... just look at the situation here. I don't know what things are like in England but surely they must be better than here. Anyway what's this woman like?'
'She's like ourselves but she's a bit fussy. I suppose being in business and that kind of thing makes her like that.'
Teresa's brother and sister brought laughter and loud banter into the house. For a long time now she had been the only one bringing home an income.
Her mother saw her going to London as a godsend. After all it was only across the water. It was not as bad as going to America. Opening her hand she surprised her mother by showing her the money she got for her dress.
'That's a lot just for one dress', said her mother. 'It's much better than working as a housemaid. There's a chance in a million that I'll get into the fashion business. I have to take the chance, don't I mam?'
'Yes, remember what you learned from your teacher, that opportunity presents itself only once?'
During the next few days Teresa and her brother and sister walked through the fields and roamed the places she used to go when she was younger. Things had changed since then. For one thing she had met her friend Mary and her brothers. She had danced with two

of them. One of them was a bit of an idiot but sadly enough he was the one she liked.

He was in jail now, so to hell with everyone and everything, she decided she's head for London. Peter will be sent to Australia, so she'd only be able to dream of what could have been and what might have been, had she got to know him a little better. Her mind would not let him go she thought of him in the jail.

If they had met sooner it would have been so easy. Her tears surprised her but she found sleep easy. After her few days at home with her family, Teresa said her goodbyes and went back to Melen's full of anxiety and hope.

Mary and Teresa went walking along the castle wall, admiring the beautiful day. The warmth of the sun kept them warm. They stood and talked in the sunny spots and watched the wild life. In the midst of their troubles they appreciated the beauty of everything around them.

Timothy spotted them standing talking. He walked round from the side of the house and acted as if he was surprised to see them.

'Hello ladies.' They looked to see the smile on his face.

'You two look a bit dull in yourselves,' he said laughing. 'Is there something wrong?'

Teresa replied: 'No, it's worse than that and I'm going back to work before Mrs. Ward misses me.'

'Alright I'll get the information from Mary.'

Timothy put his arm around her but she shrugged him away.

'Tell me what's wrong. It must be bad to put you in that humour.'

'Do you remember my brother Peter? Well he was caught by the police.'

'I thought he was gone to America.'

'He should have been but of course he delayed and delayed; now he might end up a prisoner in Australia.'

'Do you think it will be that bad Mary?'

'Of course once they get him in jail he's finished.'
'One of my friends in England was telling me a lot of criminals over here are sent to Australia as prisoners. Some of them are murderers, but others are just petty criminals. I also heard Australia is being colonised by England and they are trying to get people out there. That's why they're using it as a prison. It's a hot and barren land.'
'It sounds a terrible place to be imprisoned. I hope he's not sent there.'
'It's a pity you didn't tell me about him before Mary. I might have been able to help.'
'How could you have helped Timothy?'
'A long time ago when I was travelling home from England, I had to stay in Liverpool because of a storm. I helped a sailor back to his boat and I met his father the captain. We had a couple of drinks together. They told me that if they could ever do me a favour, I was to contact them. Their ship was called the Terranca.'
'I'll tell my brothers what you just said. It's probably too late now for any of us to do anything.'
'I think if Peter had wanted a sailing to America or even England they would have done it quietly, no one need be any the wiser. Mary you go and get Peter out of jail. I'll give you a note for the captain of the Terranca and he will get him away.'
'You know as well as I do it's most unlikely he'll ever get out of jail.'
'Anyway, what exactly did Peter do?'
'He and a couple of fellows burned the police barracks.'
Timothy began laughing. 'From what I hear that's a fairly regular occurrence around this part of the country.
He noticed her tears and a slight quiver in her voice.
'If you can get Peter out of jail and as far as the boat then you or Teresa could walk on to the boat with him late in the evening. The guard will think that Peter's

just a sailor with a lady of the night. Peter will be safely on board.'
'I wonder would my brothers trust you and your idea Timothy.'
'It's like this Mary I don't give a damn, I don't want to see Peter go to prison either for what you say. After all there was nobody badly injured. If things should work out for him let me know and we'll give it a try. Right now do you think you and I should go for a walk?'
'If I don't go back to the kitchen soon Mrs.Ward will sack me.'
He put his arm around her and kissed her.
They didn't realise they were being watched from a little window upstairs. Mary headed back to her work. What Timothy said made sense, but sadly she thought it didn't matter now.
Mary told Teresa what Timothy said.
'Well it's one method of getting him away, but you have to get him out of jail first.

Chapter 32

Peter spent the night in the barracks cell and he didn't like it one bit. Looking out the window next morning he saw it was market day, the farmers were arriving with the animals and other goods.
The dealers, were around to buy the cattle, as were the police watching various farmers they suspected of stealing. The landlords would have reported animals stolen before the market. Peter noticed there were a lot of cattle outside the jailhouse this morning. It was not the usual place for the farmers to keep their animals.
   The barracks was a large house. It had been home to the Mulvane family until it was taken over by the police. It was built of limestone, with two windows at each side of the doorway downstairs and four on the front upstairs. The cell was a special room built at the back of the house with two windows looking out on to the street. There were policemen on guard all night. Peter was able to talk out through the bars of his cell to some of the farmers.
'Why didn't you go to America when you had the chance,' shouted one of them. He seemed concerned.
'I know I should have but it's too late now.'
Peter felt like an idiot when he thought about his situation.
'Sergeant Farrell, you are a turncoat and a useless good-for-nothing,' said Peter when he saw him arriving.
'It's you Peter that's the idiot and don't forget that you're the one who's in jail. Calling me nasty names, is not going to get a stupid fool like you anywhere.' This got a great laugh from the other policemen.
This smart remark coming from an Irishman made Peter feel bad. Being here because of the English was one thing but being put down by one of your own was terrible. What kind of a man was this Mr Farrell at all,

he wondered? When he looked out the window again there was a lot of activity going on. There were men with horses and cattle just outside his window- this was not the usual place for them. There's something strange happening. The sergeant and his men heard a gunshot it came from the back of the houses across the road.

'Don't rush over their men, it could be some kind of a trap and I don't want to get shot, do you?'

'Let's lock this place and make sure this prisoner is secure before we check out what is going on over there.'

'You two go down that way,' he pointed with his right hand in the direction of an alleyway. 'I'll go up to Market Street and we'll meet at the back of the houses.'

Hearing, another shot made them hurry. They had a lot of bother staying out of the way of farmers and their cattle running towards them.

'Some mad idiot back there is shooting,' a farmer shouted as he rushed past, pointing towards the back yard of a derelict house that was occasionally used to house animals.

The sergeant could see smoke coming from the house. He and his men were reluctant to venture too close. Another two shots rang out. They proceeded with caution. By the time they arrived at the back of the house, they could see a lot of smoke coming from the building. The farmers were trying to keep their animals in check. It wasn't just a market day for cattle. Usually every month there would be a horse fair, but this was such a day more by design than usual.

All the horses were kept on this particular street and due to the smoke and the noise of the gunfire, they were becoming unstable. There were horses neighing and men were trying to keep them calm, while another loud bang didn't help things.

The police were getting closer, now they felt more at risk. Mr. Farrell was giving signals with his hands and trying to get them closer, but he noticed that his men were reluctant.

'John will you look at Farrell the idiot, waving his hands telling us to move nearer. Well I'm telling you now, let him be the one to get closer. If someone is going to get shot, better him than me.'

'I agree with you Gerry, I'm not going any further than I am, so he can wave his arms all he likes.'

They didn't like the idea of getting shot. They knew it might only happen once and that might be the last time and for what, to satisfy the English establishment.

'John I'm going through the motions of being sincere but the only reason I'm here at all is to earn a little money.'

'The way I feel Gerry is, if there's going to be anybody shot it's not going to be me. An Englishman yes. We'll wait until these boyos who are doing the shooting come out.'

Sergeant Farrell was taking stock of the situation. Things were going nicely he thought, but he didn't realise that already his men had decided to let him handle the situation and if he got a bullet, who cares?

The sergeant waved his arm and shouted loudly. 'Gentlemen, I want you to take all the animals out of here, especially the horses, the smoke is driving them crazy.'

'If you want the animals moved then move them yourself. If there's going to be a killing,' he heard a farmer saying, 'then hopefully it will be an animal.'

The sergeant weighed up the problem. He'd wait for the perpetrators of this shooting to come out of the house. The breeze caught the smoke coming from the thatched roof and fanned the flames. They could see the timber beams that held up the burning roof. Very soon there would be no roof on the building. There was a crowd of farmers and locals standing at the bottom of the street waiting to see who'd come out of the house.

The Bluebell's Mystery

The sergeant went as close as he could to the side of the building and tried to look inside. As he was about to put his nose around the corner a shot rang out, so he quickly moved back. He waved to his fellow officers to stay where they were. Whatever was taking place in the house would have to wait until the fire did its work.

Peter looked out the window of his cell when he heard the noise. He noticed a farmer walk to the window and wrap a chain around the security bars. He heard a bang at the front door. He thought it was Mr. Farrell and his officers, back. That would just, be his bad luck. At the same time he heard another shot ring out from the house across the way. He was wondering what the hell was happening, when all of a sudden he was able to see freedom through the opening in the back wall where the window used to be. Just then he heard a terrible noise behind him. As he looked to the front he could see the door of his cell going out through the front door of the building. As he was going out the back window he thought of the damage to the house and realised that if he didn't move quickly the building would fall on him. Soon there were four people around Peter and before he could move he was on the back of a plough horse and on his way. One of the farmers shouted at him:

'Don't ever let us see your face again, look at that,' he pointed at the barracks. 'You're the cause of that house being wrecked.'

They were delighted they had managed to pull off the escape and wreck the barracks as well.

After a while Peter and his helpers were in the grounds of Melen's Demesne. He knew this place belonged to an English landlord, and this was where Mary worked. He recalled the terrible rows he had with her over her working for these people. If they found out he was hiding on their land he knew he'd be caught. He wondered why they had brought him to this estate, he

The Bluebell's Mystery

didn't realise it would be the last place the police would look for an escaped prisoner.

He could see from the way things were handled that nearly every Irishman in the area was involved in his escape. Some of these people he didn't even know. He was hidden in a little hut out in the back, so remote that the owners probably didn't know it was there. Tom and his friends had planned the escape well, and there would not be any waiting around this time.

Mary heard her name being called as a young man approached her.

'Take your friend Teresa and go for a walk along that path in about two hours.' He pointed towards the pathway that Mary and Timothy walked on many times.

'Paddy Malone will meet you and he will take you to where Peter is hiding.'

'Did he get out of jail?' The surprised look on her face told the young man that she didn't know anything about the breakout.

The girls were shocked to see the state of Peter when they arrived at the hideout. His face was covered in blood and his eyes looked swollen.

'Peter you look terrible. What happened to you? Go over as far as the stream and wash the blood off your face.'

'I had a row with one of the peelers. I gave him as good as I got, lucky enough the sergeant stepped in and stopped the fight.'

A horse suddenly appeared round the bend. It seemed to come from nowhere and Timothy dismounted.

'Hello Mary, I'm surprised to see you and Teresa here, and who is that man behind the bushes?'

'That's my brother Peter.'

'What is he doing here?'

'You probably heard he escaped.'

'Yes I did and from what they said about the barracks he's lucky to be alive.'

'I told you what to do Mary, if you could manage to get him out of jail, didn't I?'
They told Peter about the ship Terrenca.

Sergeant Farrell stood back and waited for the fire to die down. By that time there was not much of the house left. The smoke from the burning roof and the gunshots had the animals half crazed. It had man and animal choked. Eventually the sergeant entered the house.
'What the hell is going on? He said, with a shocked look on his face. There's nobody here.'
'There's not even a gun to be seen. I think we've been deceived,' said one of his men.
'You may be right, but what good has burning this house done for anybody?'
'I bet something has happened back at the barracks.'
They looked at each other and started to run in that direction. When they turned the corner they spotted the door of the cell in the street. They could see the damage to the barracks, it was almost knocked to the ground and they were able to see right out through the back of the building.
A farmer walking a bullock down the street shouted. 'Hello Mr. Farrell. What happened to the barracks, some kind of an accident?' They looked at each other with a knowing smile.
'What the hell happened and what do we do now?' shouted the sergeant as he turned to one of his men. 'That smart bastard is long gone.'
Reaching out he held his colleague by the arm. 'Don't go in there the building will fall on you and then we'll have more trouble. Let's sit here and think.'
Inwardly he was delighted, the plan of escape had worked well. Nobody except himself, the O'Sheas and John Curtis were aware how it had been achieved. The way James wrapped gunpowder in rabbit skins and different amounts of clay, thereby causing the shots to

come one a little after the other. It really sounded like gunfire. We fooled everyone, he thought with pride.

Chapter 33

Tom made his way towards the Melen house he walked along the pathways of this huge estate. The tall trees arched across the path bringing darkness, and a silence that was thought - provoking.
Teresa answered his knock on the door and she was surprised to see him.
'Why did you come to see me Tom?'
'Because some time ago Mary told me you were both offered jobs in England. Peter and I are sailing to America in the next few days and you can come with us as far as Liverpool if you want.'
'Yes I will go.'
They walked round to the back of the castle, but their little sojourn didn't go unnoticed. Sandra had unexpectedly observed this meeting and was amazed to see Tom taking Teresa for a walk.
The cheek of that useless Irishman she thought. She had nice feelings for him. She had dreamed that somehow or other she'd go to America with him rather than any of her brothers. He was the one she'd have trusted to take her there. Now the good - for - nothing goes out with someone she thought was a friend. Some friend. Another Irish good –for - nothing, she decided she'd leave this place sooner than she had planned.
As the tears came she thought, perhaps this is the price one has to pay for falling in love. As she looked out the window a trap with two people was making its way to the main gate.
Tom and Teresa had made their way to the stables where one of the stable hands offered to drive Teresa home to see her parents for the last time.
 Tom made his way home. He told his father and mother the news and they were delighted when he told

them about Peter. He noticed a sadness on his mother's face.

She spoke to him saying: 'At least he's out of jail, so let's hope now that he does not have any more problems.'

Tom turned and told them that he too was thinking of heading to America with Peter.

'That's good news Tom,' said his father. 'That way you can look out for each other.'

Tom could see the delight and sorrow in their faces. His father went to the dresser and took out some money and said. 'Here divide this between the two of you.'

'I'm all right for money but I'll give it to Peter.'

That night when Tom was going to bed he felt there was sadness in the house. Times were hard but two sons leaving at the same time must be very hard on his parents. There was going to be tough changes in the next few days for them.

He rose early next morning and noticed the brightness, the sun shone as never before. Was it real, or was it just in his mind? Had all the worries of the past left him? He could not understand why his heart felt light and full of optimism.

A new adventure and a new world was waiting. Cathleen looked at him and smiled saying, 'the best of luck Tom,' as he held her close and hugged her he could see that she was about to cry. He shook hands with his father. They held hands for what seemed a long time and then they looked at each other, knowing that they'd never see each other again in this lifetime. He walked over and gave his mother a long hug, a kiss on the cheek, then hugged her again. Her tears were falling. 'Goodbye son,' she whispered in a sad voice. She kissed him gently on the cheek. 'Take care of Peter.' He felt sad as he headed towards the village.

His mother and father stood in the doorway holding each other. They watched Tom and Cathleen holding hands as she walked part of the way with him.

'There's something you don't know about me Cathleen.'
'Well you'd better tell me now Tom, because this might be the last time we'll ever be together.'
'I want you to tell our mother and father that if things work out, I will be going to America with Sandra.'
'Well I must say Tom that is a lovely surprise. God I hope you'll be happy, good luck,' she kissed him.
Letting go his hand and putting her arms around him she kissed him again and said. 'Goodbye Tom.' She stood and cried as he faded into the distance. When Tom reached the top of the valley he turned to have a last look at his home in the bend of the river. Cathleen still standing where he had left her lifted her arm in a final wave. He felt bad leaving, and he was anxious about everything.

    He arrived at the Curtis farm and collected the pony and trap and thinking about Sandra he headed to Melen's estate. He knocked on the back door.
'Hello Mrs. Ward, would you ask Mary to come down and see me please?'
She noticed his red hair and his resemblance to his sister. Tom and Mary walked close to the castle wall it sheltered them from the breeze.
'Mary I want you to come with me now, we'll collect Peter and head for the port.'
'Okay I'll go inside and tell Mrs. Ward I'll be back tomorrow.'
As he spoke he saw Sandra coming round the corner. She was wearing beautiful clothes, as though she was going somewhere special. He looked at her long fair hair, its ruffled look, and he could tell from a distance that she was upset, but he could not understand why.
Mary could see the scowl on Sandra's face as she was coming towards them.
'Sandra is upset Tom. Did you do something on her?'
"Well you do know that I went out with her?"
'I didn't know that,' said Mary laughing.

'Well you're going to know all about everything in a few minutes Mary.'
As Mary moved away she could hear Sandra's strong accent as she greeted Tom. It sounded more like a rebuff than a greeting. He was in trouble again, but then she thought…it has always been like that with Tom, but only with the police.
'Hello Tom,' said Sandra in a cool fashion. 'May I ask what are you, doing here? I suppose you have come to see Teresa Boyle?'
Instantly he realised she had seen him with Teresa and she was jealous, so he was delighted.
'You're mistaken Sandra, I wasn't with Teresa.'
'I saw you both going out in the trap.' She sounded disappointed, he knew now that she was all mixed up. He'd use this chance to torture her and get more information and try to find out how she really felt about him. He squeezed her hand as they walked along. For all her giving out he felt she still liked him and she sounded as if she was going to cry.
'The reason I called to see Teresa was, to tell her I was hopefully going to America with a girl called Sandra and it would be a great opportunity for her to travel to London to see Marion Shelton.'
'Oh, I'm sorry Tom, I got it wrong didn't I? She smiled.
'You look as though you're dressed to travel Sandra.'
'Yes, having seen you and Teresa together, I decided there was no point in staying here. I was going home.'
'I'd like to go to America with you but first I have to talk to Timothy, it's got to do with our travel arrangements.'
He held her close and kissed her and asked her to trust him that everything would work out.
Timothy arrived out to see Tom. He smiled and said, 'so you're the missing other half?'
'Yes,' said Tom.
'You were talking to Sandra just now and I noticed she'd been crying.'
'I know, she's upset.'

'Is there something going on between you two?'
'Yes, we met one evening and she spoke about going to America.'
"With you?" came, Timothy's surprised reply.
'Why not, I'm going to America and that's why I wanted to talk to you.'
'Okay I'm listening,' said Timothy, 'no doubt some kind of a favour.' At this they started laughing.
He surprised Tom by saying, 'Sandra is nice. What do you think of her?'
'She's lovely and if I get to go to America with her, I'll consider myself the luckiest man in the world.'
'Then why don't you just go?'
'That's why I came to see you.'
'What is it you want then?'
'I was going to ask you and Sandra to wait until tomorrow morning to go to the port. There is one other thing Timothy. Teresa said she wanted to go to London, so talk to her before Sandra leaves. I'm going to join the others now, so you and Sandra will not be involved in this debacle.'
'Does Sandra know anything about this debacle as you so rightfully call it?'
'She knows nothing.'
'Good, we'll keep her in the dark as much as possible.'
Tom reached out to shake Timothy's hand; he looked him in the eye and said, 'it will be alright.' 'Incidentally how do you feel about Mary? You two seem, to get along well together.'
Timothy, being younger, blushed.
'Yes we get along fine,' he said, not wanting Tom to know too much.
Timothy thought of all that was happening, he hoped things would go all right for the O'Shea's.
When he arrived back into the kitchen, he sat down at the table with Sandra and they had a mug of tea.
'So you are fond of Tom O'Shea? I accidentally found that out,' he smiled. She lowered her eyes and nodded.

'Funny how things work out isn't it? I grow to like Mary and you grow to like her brother. We're English, and they're as Irish as could be.'
'Tom noticed you were all ready to go away today.'
'Yes Timothy he did, and I am.'
'Well he asked me would you wait until tomorrow and I'll bring you as far as the port.'
'That's kind of you Timothy. Thank you.'
 He could see the glint in her eye.
'Okay Timothy if I'm going in the morning I'll go and say goodbye to your parents now.'
When will you be going back to school?'
'In another three or four weeks.'
Sandra saw Helen and Ted in the garden picking flowers.
'Hello Helen I must thank you for a wonderful holiday. I'm leaving in the morning and Timothy said he'd see me as far as the boat.'
'I'm glad you enjoyed yourself, say hello to all in England and best regards.' They shook hands.

   Tom and Mary collected Peter and young Mick Malone who would take the trap back. They hurried toward the boat. Soon they saw the ocean in the distance it was the first time any of them had seen it. The gentle moving white foaming waves, the constant changing shadows, the spray of the water as it blew in the breeze like rain. It's beauty and expanse took them by surprise, so flat so vast with its never-ending movement. The tall ship out in the harbour was in full sail. The one coming into the dock rolled through the white surf with a steady gentle motion.
'Why have we stopped Peter?'
'Just look at the beauty of all this - doesn't it make you wonder where we fit in?
'Ah sure Peter we could ask these questions and never get the answers we need.'

They stayed overnight in a farmhouse overlooking the bay. Next morning they arrived at the port and met Timothy and Sandra. Teresa was with them.

'Tom I'll go on board,' said Timothy, and explain the situation.'

He was greeted by the captain and his son, they took him into their cabin for a drink. When he told them about Peter's escape and his predicament, Captain Ellickson said laughing.

'Another one, this happens regularly in this country.'

'I won't be sailing with you this time but maybe sometime in the future,' said Timothy.

'Anytime it favours you so be it.'

They finished their drinks and John Ellickson went back to meet the girls. He turned to Peter and said.

'You hold Sandra's hand and walk with me and Teresa, that is your name isn't it?' she nodded.

'Sandra you and Timothy keep chatting and walk with us. As they passed the guard they spoke loudly and everyone laughed. To the guard this was a regular occurrence, a couple of sailors with two attractive looking ladies

After a while Tom joined the queue and went on board. Timothy on his way off the ship just nodded to him as they passed. He joined Mary who was crying, but he could see she was happy. They sat and watched the people going on board, and they knew that most of them would never come back to Ireland again.

As the ship moved away from the pier Tom and Peter looked back at Mary and Timothy. Tom felt sad that she was not going with them, but the fact that Timothy was standing by her side made him feel better. Peter's loneliness took him back to the time he was fighting with Mary.

Sandra stood beside Tom and she could see the sadness on his face. The people took their last look at Ireland as though they were losing a part of themselves.

The Bluebell's Mystery

'Tom, what was all the secrecy at Melen's, when you asked me to wait, remember?'
'You didn't know what was going on Sandra. Peter had just escaped from jail, so we had to get him out of the country.'
'So that's what all the mystery was about?'
'We didn't want you or Timothy to be involved.'
The ship docked at Liverpool and it was going to be there for a couple of days. The police came looking to see were there any undesirables on board seeing as the ship had come from Ireland, but the O'Shea's had just left.
The four of them went as far as London, Sandra's people were very surprised when she introduced Tom to them.
'So you're going to America with an Irishman?'
'Yes mother, I am, and you know something, I feel great.'
They stayed for a day, Sandra's mother was happy for her. Soon they had to leave. When they sailed out of Liverpool, Sandra held Tom close and shed a tear. Her only consolation now was this Irishman beside her. Teresa went to see Marion Shelton and worked in the fashion industry. Peter stayed in England and worked in the clothing business.

On their journey back from the port Mary turned to Timothy saying, 'Everything went well, it was great to see Peter on board the ship. I will miss my brothers. Did you see the look on Sandra's face when she saw Tom? I'm sure she turned away and started to cry.'
'I can understand that, because I was talking to her a few times and the conversation always came round to discussing Tom.'
'There's no doubt about it Timothy, she fancies him, what's the word... she's besotted by him.' That got them laughing.

'What's going to happen to me now that my brothers and my friend Teresa are gone?.
'Well, first Cathleen is going to get married before she goes off, and I'm hoping to be asked to the wedding. A short while after that, sadly enough, I'm going back to finish my schooling. When I have my exams done I'm coming back here and then you and I will head off.'
Their journey was slipping away, and Mary's thoughts took her back to when the ship was pulling away from the pier. The terrible sadness of the people and the loss of her brothers made her cry. She was not going to have a friend like Teresa at work, and she was going to miss her, that along with her secret was beginning to take its toll on her. It took her all her time to keep from crying in front of Timothy. With the rolling motion of the trap and the clippity clop of the horse, Mary was soon fast asleep. Timothy put a coat over her. He looked at her red hair. It was a little dishevelled and it made her look very attractive. He noticed the peaceful look on her face, making him want to hold her close. He loved her, this he knew, but it was not the right time to tell her he thought. He'd hold on another while, although it tugged at his heart. They'd go to America where he'd marry her, but as yet it was too soon to move in that direction.
The miles quickly rolled past and Mary was brought back to reality with a gentle shake. She felt chilly, they stood close, the horse moved to eat a bit of grass, and the sway made them fall against each other. He kissed her and said everything went well today. They parted, he to the stables, she to the house.
Mrs.Ward met Mary and asked. 'Well did things go all right today? Here drink this and tell me everything child, did they get away?'
Mary nodded; 'Yes they did.'
'You do know Mary that ship stops over in Liverpool for a couple of days.'
'Yes, Timothy told me.'

'Was Teresa going to London to see Mrs. Shelton, or was she going to America with Peter?' asked Mrs. Ward.
'To be honest Mrs.Ward all that matters is that they got away safely. I'm very tired, I must go to bed.'
Mrs.Ward laughed and said, 'You're right Mary, you've had a full day, goodnight.'
On her way to bed Mary thought of what Mrs. Ward had said. 'Is everything all right child? It was a strange thing for her to say. Soon sleep gave her comfort.

Chapter 34

Sargeant Farrell was called in front of a police board of inquiry. 'Mr. Farrell, you do realise why you and your officers have been called here today?'

'Yes I do I have been told.'

'Well as you know we are here to determine if you are guilty of negligence or was there some ulterior motive.'

'What makes you think that there might have been any other motive? I've been working for the police for many years and there has never been any problems.'

'That's exactly why this enquiry is taking place. We are going to find out if there was a problem with your behaviour on that day. Why did you find it necessary to leave your prisoner unguarded?'

Patrick considered this man's attitude to be that of a snotty-nosed snob. He stated firmly. 'Which was the most important, that somebody might have been shot or a prisoner who was locked in a cell might escape... Perhaps you could answer that for me?'

'I'm not here to answer your questions Patrick,' he said in a sneery way. 'You're here to answer mine and don't forget that.'

'In that case then maybe you'd try and be a little more civil,' Patrick said.

The chairman of the inquiry interrupted saying:

'You two will have to adopt a more positive attitude towards each other in order to get this problem sorted.' They agreed to his suggestion.

'We are here to see were you Patrick as an officer in Her Majesty's Police Force, doing your job properly.'

'Then perhaps you should ask the policemen who were with me, what do they think?'

'I intend doing just that, I'd be obliged if you would step down now and let your associate Mr. Connolly take your place.'

'Mr. Connolly, perhaps you would explain to us exactly what happened on that day?'

'We heard the noise of gunfire and Mr. Farrell told us we'd better check and see what was happening. He told us to lock up the prisoner in his cell which we did and we secured the barracks.'

The two officers told exactly the same story.

As much as the Board tried, they were not able to put the blame on Mr. Farrell or any of his officers.

'Mr. Farrell, will you step up here again please? He indicated with his hand. 'Do you realise Patrick that one house was pulled down and another house was burnt down.'

At this Patrick started laughing and this caused the listening fraternity to giggle. The Board were not pleased.

'We have come to the conclusion that you are partly responsible for this incident getting out of hand. You could have left one of your men back at the barracks with the prisoner. If you had done that, we might still have our prisoner today, isn't that right?'

'I locked the barracks and made sure that it was secure. I then proceeded with my men to where the shooting was taking place.'

'Aha! Patrick but there was no shooting.'

'It's alright for you to say that now, but it was the sound of gunfire that we heard and my police officers have verified what I am saying. So there's no sense in blaming me for what might have happened or what could have happened. I did what I thought was necessary at the time and that's all I could do.'

After two hours of a recess, the Chief of Police issued an order that Patrick and two of his men be suspended indefinitely.

Patrick was thinking how he liked being in the police force. He was getting paid by the English and at the same time was able to help his fellow Irishmen. He went back to his little house along the Morta road and said goodbye to his few friends. He'd had enough of working undercover as a policeman, so by the time his suspension was over he'd be gone.

Chapter 35

Mary woke to an empty room it was now that she missed Teresa most. However, she brushed her sadness aside, because she had to get her more immediate problem sorted.
This was her weekend off she was glad to be going home. When she arrived, she related all the details about Tom and Peter getting away to her parents and her sister. She could see the relief on their faces, mixed with an air of sadness.
'Cathleen, have you decided on a particular day for your wedding?'
'Yes it's going to be in two weeks time. This time it's definite, we are not changing our minds, you can be sure of that. You can bring any friends you want. The priest is coming and he'll marry us on Saturday morning. Ther will be music and dancing, let's hope the weather favours the situation, a little better than it is now.'
'Did you try mother's wedding dress and coat on you yet? How do they look?'
'There were a few alterations to be done but it looks well now. I'll show you the changes we made.' Cathleen held the dress up against here body and said. 'Do the alterations show that my dress- making is as good as yours and Teresa's?'
Mary started laughing. 'It looks lovely Cathleen, and yes your dressmaking is just as good.'
As they walked towards the river, Mary pointed out her hand saying: 'Look Cathleen, is that an otter or a water hen?'
'I'm not sure but these bushes are a haven for all kinds of little animals. Jim is going to sell off the bit of land he owns. No doubt that's going to delay us for a while and then we'll head off.'

'Has he arranged to get land over there for you?'

'Yes he has, we're lucky you know. What are you going to do now that Teresa is gone Mary, will you go over and join her in London? You should, you would enjoy the fashion business, I can see that from your sketches.'

'I'm going to wait a while and see what news we'll get from Tom and Peter. I might go to America with you yet.'

Mary knew she was telling a white lie. No matter what happened she'd have to wait until her baby was born. She wouldn't tell Cathleen yet, as it might cause her to change her plans.

The days at home passed quickly. Mary arrived back to work, but in her heart she knew her enthusiasm had gone from her workplace with her friend Teresa.

Mary and Timothy went for long walks. They enjoyed each other's company and they wanted to be together. Over all this hung the shadow that he had to go away again. Mary's tears flowed freely when she thought of this. Her parting from her brothers and her friend and now the one she loved, plus the fact she was carrying his child made her feel lonely. She had to try and hide this from him, although she felt tempted to tell him. It might stop him going back to finish his schooling and he so close to his dream of being an engineer, so she decided she would not tell him. The days passed quickly and the wedding day was getting close. Mary, attending to her chores in the kitchen, caught the lady's attention by saying. 'Cathleen is getting married this Saturday and if any of you ladies, including you Mrs. Ward would like to come to the house, you are all welcome.'

Timothy secured a horse and trap on the morning of the wedding. He collected Mary and laughing he said to her. 'We'll make this a day to remember, I like your dress and the flower in your hair - you do look pretty.'

Mary wore a knitted coat over her blue dress. This was the coat she thought she'd never get to wear. She had been knitting it since she was young. It had a high collar and a neat belt around the waist.
He clipped the reins and away they went at a frisky pace. Mary studied the pony. He was brown with a speck of white on his head and on one of his fetlocks. His mane hung down along his neck. He looked nice and he seemed happy in what he was doing. She looked at Timothy and he smiled. They knew their time was running out, another week and he would have to go, and then it was back to loneliness for herself. The pony trotted along as if he knew he was going to a wedding.
'Stop when we're at the top of the hill Timothy and look down into the valley, look at the beauty of the landscape.'
He felt the stillness of the morning, with the sun still making an effort to come out from behind the clouds. He could see the overgrown hedges, the hideout of the fox, the badger and the pheasant.
'We better keep going Timothy before the rain catches up with us.'

They arrived at the O'Shea's house and Timothy was taken back a little by the fact that everybody wanted to shake his hand. He didn't realise that these people knew he'd been part of, or was involved in Peter's escape.
Cathleen wore the coat and dress her mother had worn on her wedding day. The hat and the scarf she wore across her shoulders were made from fox fur and she looked young, elegant and beautiful. Her hair was pulled back and clipped neatly so that it hung partly across her shoulders.
Soon the music started and Timothy danced with the bride.
'When are you going back to England?'

'I have to go in a weeks time.'
'I think Mary will be missing you then. Indeed I think I will miss her myself.'
'Did you enjoy you're stay here?'
'Yes I had a great time and don't forget I was also involved in a bit of intrigue,' he laughed.
When the dance finished he said: 'Thank you for inviting me to your wedding, and may I wish you and Jim every happiness.' He politely said goodbye.
'You know something mother, Mary has met a nice fellow, even though he's English, he's courteous and polite.'
She commented to her husband Jim. 'It's a strange one, Mary is with an Englishman, and Tom just went to America with an English girl. Don't things work out in peculiar ways?'
'Strange is the word. I never thought I'd be going to America with such a good looking bride as you.' They hugged each other tightly and felt the confidence and pleasure of their union and the optimism of beginning a new life together thousands of miles from home.
The wedding was enjoyed by all. Mary and Timothy arrived back at his home, and her workplace. After a few joyful days, and this being their last night together she knew that she could no longer keep her secret.
'Timothy, I was reluctant to tell you before you left but I feel I have to now.' Her tears were falling freely.
He held her close. 'Don't cry Mary, tell me what is the matter?'
'I'm going to have your baby Timothy.'
'How long have you known this?'
'I've been aware of it for weeks.'
'Why in heaven's name didn't you tell me before now? Anyway stop crying, this is my child and I'm delighted.'
He put his arms round her, held her and told her he loved her. They agreed he should go back to England and finish his schooling and then come back for her and they'd head for America.

He kissed her again and said: 'I have to leave now Mary.'
It was now that she felt a loneliness she'd never known before. All her friends were gone, so Mary slowly cried herself to sleep.

As the weeks went by she could see her body changing. It was something she could not hide any longer, so she gave up trying. It became apparent to everyone that Mary was pregnant. To become pregnant out of wedlock in Ireland at this time was to bring disaster on oneself and one's family.
It was treated as though one had committed the gravest sin. It was so bad that girls usually tried to hide it from their parents.
She decided that she was not going to succumb to a lot of this nonsense. She knew that a lot of the people understood her situation better than she did. These people had seen children die, and there was not a family among them who in some way had not experienced death. To see life coming into the world was a great happening. It should make people look to God and ask questions and wonder what was it all about. People, know that life goes on just the same.

Mary had a visit from Timothy's mother in her bedroom one evening.
'I'd like to have a talk with you Mary.'
Helen sat down beside her on the bed. I can see that you're pregnant and I have a good idea who the father is, but if you don't want to tell me that's all right.'
'You are right in what you are thinking Mrs. Melen. What, should I do now?' she was starting to cry.
'That's the very question I was going to ask you Mary.' Then they both started to laugh. Mary's laughter soon turned to tears again, and after a while she was crying her heart out on Helen's lap. Cuddling Mary like this, Helen wondered what would she do if this girl was her own daughter. She made up her mind that she'd treat her as if she was. She could feel Mary's sobs so she sat

and caressed her as she cried and cried. Helen covered her with the bedclothes and told her to have a good rest.

Turning to leave she whispered in a motherly way. 'Don't cry Mary, everything will be alright you'll see. Your baby is my grandchild you know.' This made Helen feel good, so she began wondering what name they'd call the child. Mary missed Timothy. She thought that when she needed him most, he was not around. She was happy that she had told him before he went back to England. Sometimes she would have dark thoughts. All Timothy had to do was to catch the boat to America and she'd never see him again. At night when she was alone, thinking like this would see her crying in her room until sleep would come and give her much needed relief. Other men had been in the same situation, had left and never came back. She knew Timothy would not do that to her, yet her mind would not let the dark thoughts go - it was breaking her heart.

Chapter 36

Tom and Sandra were delighted to be on their way and enjoying their courtship at the same time. Everyone thought they were married it suited the two of them. As far as they were concerned they were. They wondered did God hate them, the way the sea was behaving they thought He was out to drown all on board the ship. The waves looked mountainous the way they were running. It seemed as if they were in the hands of a giant and he was going to shake them to death.

One minute they were at the top of a wave, then they'd drop to what seemed a thousand feet. Their stomachs would come down after them. They didn't realise that they could be so sick and still be alive. They'd have the occasional good spell, get strong again and then back to storms and sickness.

Tom marvelled at the sailors. For them to live this kind of life they had to be mighty men. They heard a shout: 'Look over there, that's land!' Everyone looked in that direction. Some of the people put their hands up to their eyes to shade the sun. The land looked vague in the distance but it was there. It caused a great feeling among these people who had been battered around for so long and who thought that the word 'land' was gone forever. They looked in shocked silence. They knew it was not England or Ireland but a whole different world, somewhere else on earth.

Tom and Sandra looked around at their fellow travellers. Some of them were laughing while some were crying. At last they could see great happiness. They had survived the terrible sea, and nothing would ever frighten them again. Between the torture of the

Famine and the sea and to be alive still, what could possibly beat them now?

When Tom and Sandra stepped ashore, he held her hand as they walked in this new land of total freedom, something that he had never known back home in Ireland under English rule and oppression. As they walked along he thought of the strangeness of things. He stood and looked into Sandra's eyes and said. 'Here I am receiving my freedom from England, after a lifetime of being ruled by that country. Now I'm going to ask an English girl to marry me and again be ruled by the English. You know I do love you Sandra.'
'Yes I do Tom, I love you too and I'll marry you as soon as we see a minister. Oh, and thanks for accepting the fact that you are going to be ruled by me, you can call me your Queen!' They kissed. Word eventually came to the O'Shea household from the Denver area of Colorado that they had got married and owned a farm.
James and Rose were happy and felt good for both of them. His father said with a tear. 'No more stealing, isn't it great dear?'

Mary approached Mrs. Melen saying: 'I'm going home for the weekend, it's been three weeks since I was home last.'
'It's a long walk for you Mary, I'll get the horse and trap and I'll drive you home. It's a grand day anyway.'
Mary was glad because she was beginning to feel the strain of carrying her child.
When they arrived at Mary's home and introductions had been made, the two ladies got talking, as older women are likely to do.
'Have a drink of tea or would you prefer a drop of poteen?' said Rose.
'I'll settle for a cup of tea, thank you.'
They discussed Mary's predicament and the wisdom and maturity of both women put the whole debacle into

its proper place - young people cannot be watched these times.'

'The Catholic Church will no doubt frown on such a happening,' said Helen. They laughed.

'What would they know anyway, they're all men,' said Rose.

After having her tea Helen was handed a drink of poteen. 'This tastes very good, it tastes as good as some of the drink we had at our week of celebrations. You do realise Rose that your daughter is quite a dress designer.'

'Yes I saw some of the sketches she made, and I hope her talent benefits her in the future. What's going to happen to her now?'

'She'll have our grandchild and life will go on as it always does.'

When they looked across at Mary, she was asleep on the cot in the corner.

'Rose, I'd be obliged if you'd tell Mary to stay at home until the baby is born. Walking to work is getting too much for her. I'll be back to see her soon, and of course she'll be paid until her child is born.'

The ladies hugged and parted.

Mary woke to find her mother sitting beside her, crying.

'Mother I'm sorry I've brought shame on our family.'

'Don't talk nonsense Mary, do you realise this child will be my first grandchild? Have you decided on a name yet?'

'No, I didn't think about that.'

'Well the main thing now is you're not to worry.'

When Cathleen arrived home Mary discussed her problem with her.

'I bet I know who the father is.'

'You're right Cathleen, it is Timothy. His mother drove me home today. All she seems to be concerned about is that the baby is her grandchild.'

'What will happen now Mary?'

'When Timothy finishes College he's coming back to collect me and we will go to America. When are you going to venture out Cathleen?'

'We'll wait until Jim gets the farm sold off, although that might take a bit of time.'

The joys of springtime seem to make the weeks go by quickly. Mary was missing Timothy and that terrible thought still haunted her mind. Was she destined to stay here on this farm for the rest of her life alone with only her child for company? Had she made the greatest mistake a young girl can make and would she spend her life paying the terrible price? Could this happening make Timothy go on alone, perhaps never seeing his child? As she walked down along the river she cried to herself... life could be so cruel.

Mary was on her way back towards the house when she began to feel sick, so she walked faster. There was something strange happening inside her and it had to do with her child. She saw her mother and Cathleen in the distance.

'Mother quickly,' she shouted.

Her mother came running and called Cathleen, soon they had Mary in the house lying on the cot.

'Cathleen you go for Mrs. McNally she'll know what to do, go now hurry! Mary's going to have her baby, it's too early but then when did babies ever care?'

Rose was worried things were happening too soon, because she'd had experiences of things she did not like to think about. Back in her day some premature babies did not make it, so she prayed and hoped.

Mrs. McNally arrived at the house and her attitude and manner put her straight into the position of authority. Cathleen and her mother obeyed her every word. Mary worked at giving birth.

Chapter 37

When Timothy arrived back in England he was aware that life had taken on a different meaning. He thought about Mary all the time, and what exactly he should do. He felt that all of a sudden maturity was taking a hold of him. Although he was almost twenty and still at school he had to take on the attitude of a man. After a few weeks he decided he'd go and see Teresa Boyle in Shelton's clothes premises. He was delighted to see her but he got a surprise when he saw Peter O'Shea.
'Hello Peter I see you didn't bother going on to America after all.'
'No I didn't Timothy, I got myself a job here in the clothes business so I decided to stay.'
'Did Tom go on to America with Sandra?'
'Yes he did.'
'Well how are you getting on in the fashion business Teresa?'
'I'm delighted I came, because I find the work interesting.'
He realised they didn't know that Mary was pregnant so he didn't tell them.

Timothy attended his college with an enthusiasm he'd never shown before. At last his schooling was finished. He had to make a decision, should he go back home or take the college's offer of staying on another two months to secure a distinction on top of his engineering degree? He decided against his will to stay on, and the two months went quickly. Soon he was heading for Liverpool with his friends from college. They both were going to America and were trying to persuade him to go with them.
'Hey Timothy, come on with us we'll start an engineering business over there ourselves.'

They had him in an undecided predicament. He thought about Mary and their baby. He could jump on a ship and go to America, but he wondered would it be the best thing to do. Timothy admired the beautiful landscapes and the old type architecture as the coach rolled along. He probably would never come back this way again. They arrived at Liverpool, and his friends persuaded him to board the ship with them. She was a big boat, and the three of them leaned across the side and watched the people coming on board. Timothy's mind was telling him that he should not to be here.

'Timothy,' said Eric, 'America will be a whole new experience. I believe in the civil engineering business there are bridges and buildings being constructed on a scale that we haven't even dreamed of. Nothing here can be compared to what they are doing over there. One of the professors was telling us they are building bridges over rivers with spans we can only begin to imagine. It will be a great experience.'

Chapter 38

After what seemed an eternity Mary had her baby. Mrs.McNally took the child and held her in her arms, the baby didn't cry, there was no sign of life. The midwife tried in vain to stir life from the child but it was no use. Mary realised that Mrs. McNally was not bringing the baby to her and she wondered why. When her mother put her arms around her Mary started to cry, she knew at once, she cried hysterically. Her mother stayed with her and was happy when Mary fell asleep for what seemed a long time.

Cathleen and her mother looked after Mary as though she was a child herself. Mary's father in those sad days made a tin box and wrapped the tiny body in cloth. He then made a bag from hide and wrapped the tiny body again and put it in the box coffin The whole affair brought a sadness to the O'Shea household that they had never experienced before. After a week Mary was strong enough to take the box and the body of her child to a quiet little place and bury her. She knelt and prayed with her family.

'What do you think you'll do now Mary, what's going to happen? It looks like Timothy is not coming back here.'

'I know Cathleen, he should have been here two weeks ago and that's giving him a week or so to spare. I'm going to stay here until I get strong enough to travel. If you and Jim are here much longer I'll go with you, if not then I will travel on my own.'

Cathleen could see a determination in Mary that she'd never seen before, an independence that said she would not depend on anyone ever again. This tough determination brought sadness to Cathleen and she could see that it brought out feelings in her sister that she did not like.

'Wouldn't it be amazing Cathleen if I went on my own and met Timothy over there?'
'That would cause you more and bigger problems Mary. Perhaps you would do better to forget about him?'
The words went through Mary's heart like a knife and she started to cry. Cathleen hugged her, and crying said. 'Oh! God Mary, what a troubled life this is.' They made their way back home.
Mary got a shock when she saw a horse and trap outside the house. She turned to Cathleen with excited eyes and said: 'Timothy's here, come on!'

Chapter 39

Mary's disappointment was obvious to Cathleen, and the tears welled in her eyes when she realised it wasn't Timothy. Helen Melen did not know how disappointed Mary was. She had arrived at the O'Shea house and was badly shaken when she heard the news about her grandchild.
'Hello Mary, I'm sorry about your baby,' she said, giving her a hug, she cried.
'Did you hear from Timothy?'
'I didn't hear anything yet Mary, but he should have been home by now. Perhaps he got delayed somehow. What name did you call your baby?'
'I called her Rosie after my mother.'
They chatted for a while again Helen extended her sorrow to Mary and then took her leave, wondering about Timothy.
The weeks went by quickly and Mary could feel her body getting stronger. Her thoughts were starting to focus on America. She wondered should she try to go out to Tom and Sandra, although it seemed very far. She'd travel with Cathleen and her husband - at least she'd have their company. When she thought of Timothy she felt so let down she always had a tear. She knew that even if she left Ireland on her own and met him in America or England by accident, she wouldn't be able to forgive him, even though she'd very much like to. She made her way to where she had buried her child. She stood and prayed and talked about her problems.
'You know something Rosie,' she said, 'I miss your father, but I don't think he's going to come back for me, although it would be wonderful if he did. She was crying and trying to wipe her tears away at the same time. You know I really miss him.'

She dropped down on to her knees and cried for a long time. She felt stronger then she was, and her sojourns with her child seemed to take away her problems. As she stood up she laughed at the way she was dressed, in an old pair of Peter's trousers, a jersey and an old jacket belonging to one of the boys. She said goodbye to her baby and headed back to the house.

Mary's mother could see that she was getting very fit and was delighted that Mary would have her sister to travel with. She thought, what a pity, that Timothy boy didn't come back for Mary. He didn't realise it but he had destroyed things for the two of them. Rose had seen them at the wedding and could see the way they looked at each other. She realised that age and time could not wear love away, of that she was sure. She wiped away the tear before she answered the knock on the door.

She stood back and said 'Hello' and pointed down towards the river. Mary was making her way back to the house and noticed Jim or her father coming towards her in the fading light of a dull evening. She decided to hide and jump out and give them a shock. As they passed the corner of the shed she shouted loudly, Whooooo-a! He jumped back with the fright. Timothy turned to face who shouted and saw Mary, who on seeing him couldn't hold herself together. She began to fall, but he put his arms around her, and she cried for a long time. To keep her from crying hysterically, he held her close and he could feel every throb of her body.

'I thought you were not coming back - you should have told me.'

'I stayed on longer at college to benefit my exams that's why I was delayed Mary.'

He felt her closeness and was happy to see she was delighted to see him. She gently pushed him away, saying, 'You know Timothy the baby arrived

prematurely and due to some kind of complication she was dead at birth.'
'I'm sorry I wasn't here for the birth. I thought I'd be back in time forgive me please.'
'Our daughter is buried up there on the little hill not far from the river,' she whispered in a very low tearful tone. It's too dark now to go there but I'll show you tomorrow.'
'Tell me Mary what name did you give her?'
'I called her Rosie after my mother.'
She began crying again and saying how sorry she was that something went wrong and that she had done no wrong.
He kissed her and said, 'I know Mary, stop crying.' He wiped her tears and after a while he noticed her clothes and said, 'I like your style.' She laughed. 'So you should I made them myself.'
Their closeness reminded them of their time in the woods laughing and kissing, as if nothing had changed. They knew they would never part again.

Mary's mother was so excited when Cathleen and Jim arrived home that they asked her what had happened. 'Did you by any chance find a piece of gold in the garden beside your roses mother?'
Just then James stepped in. 'You'll never guess who has arrived? She'll be here in a few minutes.'
'It must be someone important the way you're fussing about.'
'Is it possible it could be the doctor's wife?' said James with a smile.
They were left playing the guessing game a little longer. At last the door opened and Mary walked in, but she was ignored. They all were waiting to see who the other lady was, when Timothy stepped in. He saw the surprised look on Cathleen's face and he realised they thought he was not coming back for Mary. He didn't tell them he was on board the ship that was heading to

America and when he saw a sailor going to pull the gangplank he walked off, waved to his two friends and told them to stay in touch. A little further down along the quay he boarded a ship to Ireland. Now he knew it was the best thing he had done.

Timothy could feel the delight in everyone, but at the same time he felt as if he was one of them, easy going, relaxed and yet with a self- determination that could only come from their experience of terrible times and troubles. The talk, the poteen, the laughter, soon Mary and Timothy were on their own again, everyone had gone to bed.

Mary's mother came into the kitchen in the morning to find Timothy asleep on the cot in the corner and Mary asleep with her arm across his chest. It brought a tear and memories of when she was young and not long married. After their breakfast Timothy took Mary's hand and said. 'Come on, we'll go visit our daughter's grave.'

They stayed for a little while and said a prayer.

It was a sad occasion for them but in their minds they knew their world was waiting. Timothy enjoyed his stay at the O'Shea home, and he visited his daughter's grave a few times. Mary took him to some of the secret places that she and her friends had haunted in their younger days. He enjoyed the few days he spent with the O'Shea's, now it was time for him to go home.

It was a beautiful morning as they walked and enjoyed the countryside. The wildness, the untouched beauty, the birds and the rabbits, life was as full as it always had been. It was only one's troubles that dulled things. They talked of America and how soon they could leave.

Timothy's mother was taken back when she saw them standing in the sitting room. She gave Timothy a hug, and he explained to her why he had been delayed. He spoke about his child and that he and Mary, were planning to leave for America soon.

The Bluebell's Mystery

'Are you going to get married?'

'Yes we are but not here, we'll wait until we get to America.'

Helen walked to the cupboard, opened the drawer and took out a small box.

'I'd like you to have this Timothy. This is my mother's wedding ring. I hope it brings you and Mary good luck.' She kissed them both on the cheek. Timothy's father interrupted, saying: 'I assume you'll stay here a while and we will have a shindig, as you Irish like to call it Mary.'

He then walked over and shook her hand. She had only met him on a few occasions.

'Timothy,' his mother said laughing. 'I take it that your future wife will not be going back to her old job in the kitchen. You will help Mary organize the festivities won't you Timothy we'll make it a great wedding party.'

'Of course we will,' Mary smiled. I'm going to see Mrs. Ward and the girls in the kitchen.'

Helen saw how Timothy held her hand, and walked with her. After hearing their story Mrs. Ward said: 'It is no great surprise, we have been expecting this. When is the party and when are you going to leave?'

She hugged Mary and wished her all the luck in the world.

'What's the word on Teresa and Peter?'

'I paid a visit sometime ago to Teresa,' said Timothy. She is working for Mrs. Shelton in London and loves it. I was surprised to meet Peter there, he stayed with her.'

Mrs. Ward began to laugh.

The preparations for their going away party were as exciting as the preparations for the ball.

The O'Shea's, the Melen's and a lot of Mary's friends danced, feasted and drank to their heart's content. It was a happy and a sad occasion for both families.

Within a week or so Mary and Timothy arrived at the port. Walking along the quay together, Mary gave Timothy a nudge saying: 'Look quickly', her

outstretched arm pointing at the rainbow in the middle of the harbour and a tall ship about to sail through it.
'Isn't that beautiful?'
The colours pink, white and yellow and green mixed together to shock one's eye with its beauty. As this scene was taking place Mary said: 'Timothy, we'll follow the rainbow to its end in America, that's where our crock of gold lies.'
He laughed and gave her a kiss.
'Will you marry me, Mary?'
'Oh! Yes I will,' he kissed her again. 'That's for good luck. Lets hope it stays with us to the end of the rainbow.'
They hugged each other.
On their way and having a last look back at Ireland, the captain of the ship walked towards Timothy and shocked Mary when he said:
'Timothy Melen do you take Mary O'Shea to be, your lawfully wedded wife?'
'Yes I do.'
'Mary O'Shea do you take Timothy Melen to be, your lawfully wedded husband?'
'I do.'
He put his grandmother's ring on her finger and kissed her. Cathleen and Jim along with their fellow travellers clapped and cheered. They followed their rainbow to its end in America, to find as Mary had said their crock of gold.

Chapter 40
Matthew

Matthew decided to go to the Catholic Hall early. He played a few games of billiards downstairs before going to the dance. He loved to hear the music and the noise of the dancing overhead, as he played his games of snooker.
There was a good crowd and he loved the buzz... the bright lights and the style of the girls with their different coloured dresses. It was what most young men dreamed about, a hall full of lovely girls and music that would lift one's soul and instil an anticipation of meeting an attractive girl. Daft, thinking why not.
When the band started playing a waltz, Matthew nudged his friend Pat in the elbow. 'Watch these two dancing they're great. They are real professional ballroom dancers.' It was an exhibition that Matthew loved. Ballroom dancing appealed to him, he'd have loved to do this, but alas.
He enjoyed this time with his friends, and he took a girl for a walk. After a while they parted company.
He walked towards home, hoping to get a lift but it was not to be. It was a cold dark night, he was thinking of the girl he just left. He saw someone on the road in front of him this was the spot he hated most. He turned to run but as he did so, that someone or something, was still facing him. He turned again but it was getting closer. He felt the blood rushing to his head. He was about to cry out for help, when he realised he was standing next to a gate into a field. He jumped over it. He heard the sound of cloth ripping and he felt his trousers being torn. That bloody farmer and his barbed wire. What the hell is going on here? Someone is trying to frighten me and the rotten dog is succeeding.

The sudden cold of the wet puddle he stepped into shocked him. Looking behind he could see that 'it' the thing, was still there and getting closer. He moved as fast as he could through another gap, but he felt the soreness in his ankle. He came to a stream he knew where he was or at least he thought he did. He slowed down. Whoever or whatever it was, he had lost him or it. As he was about to pull himself together the thing started to come at him again.
Matthew dashed across the river getting soaked. Wiping his face he got the taste of blood, and he felt the soreness of the briar that scraped his hand. He dashed around the ditch to try and hide from the silvery shadow of a man or ghost, or some bastard of a thing that had him terrified.
He prayed as he ran through the hedge. He felt the thorns slice into his hands and face. Surely it would not follow him in here? At least the morning was starting to get brighter, although in this ring of trees it was dark, the thing had followed him. He felt he was trapped. If he was going to be attacked it was going to be now. He moved into the circle a little further and fell on to his knees. He put his head on to the ground, almost splitting his forehead on a stone. With his eyes closed and locked in prayer, he waited for the blow that would finish him. He put his hands tightly around the stone, stood up quickly, turned and threw it at this ghost of a thing, as hard as he could. He dropped down again quickly, only to hit his head on something soft. He put his hands over his face and waited. He knew he had no chance now but he also knew if the vision was human he'd see someone lying on the ground. A blow from a stone so big would kill a human. After a while of silence he opened his eyes and he could see the bright sky blinking through the hedge.

That something under his nose felt soft. He looked around for the ghost. It seemed to be gone thank God, he thought. He stood up, wiped his face with his hands and saw the blood on his clothes. He then recognised where he was, he was inside the ring where he had seen the bluebells years ago. He put his hands into the hole in the ground and lifted out a box. It was small with some kind of a skin wrapped around it, Matthew pulled this away. It was wrapped again in a waxed leathery type skin. Something strange was going on. He thought he'd found treasure, or someone or something had shown it to him. A while ago he was terrified, but now he was quite calm and hoped he'd found something of great value. He looked fearfully around to see had the ghost really gone, only to see the girl he had imagined seeing here on his adventure with his pals when they followed the river through the caves. Again he saw her long coat, her collar turned up and a knitted type hat pulled down on her long red hair, laced up shoes, a long bright dress. It was the same girl, so why was he not afraid He watched her and wondered what was happening. He held out the box to her as if to say, 'look what I found.' After a while she faded away and he was alone. Looking closer into the box he found a note in a wallet. He put the box under his arm, he pulled his collar up and licked the blood from his hand. As he stepped out of the circle he glanced back to see the shimmering light through the hedge glisten on the stream.

   He made his way home, quietly changed his clothes, cleaned up and over a mug of tea told his mother the story.
'Matthew, I'm serious now, were you drinking last night?'
'I knew you'd think that mam, but let's read the letter and we'll know everything.'
'Okay Matthew.'
His mother unfolded the letter and read it out loud.
'Hello, in this box is the remains of my child who was born lifeless. It is not allowed for her to be buried in consecrated soil at this time. This bothers me, perhaps

in later years things will have changed in Ireland. When you, anybody who finds this letter, please inter my daughter Rosie in a graveyard. I'm going to America and I may not get back. Thank you Mary O'Shea.'
'You know Matthew this is a very strange happening, why do you think it happened to you?'
'I honestly don't know but I must admit mam that I've always been afraid walking home from the town at night. As you know it's been said in this house that there was a ghost on the bray...a hill on the way into town. This happening proves to me mam that there was something strange there.'
'It's an eerie kind of situation isn't it? Does it bother you in any way Matthew?'
'No, not really.'
He noticed his mother cry.
'We'll have to do what the letter says.'
'How in heaven's name mam are we going to do that?'
'Your uncle's cousin is a priest. We'll tell him the story and he will bury the child.'
'Yes Matthew,' said the priest with a satisfactory smile. We can solve the problem okay but you and your friends will have to do a little tidying up in the old graveyard for me. It's there since before the years of the Famine.'
'Do you know something Pat, this priest is no fool, he's using this scenario to get us to tidy up the graveyard. Little does he know we looked into our family tree here not so long ago ourselves.
'Look over there in the corner where the gravestones are lying down, do you notice anything?'
'Yes I do, I bet you're going to ask me did I notice the wild roses. Well I did and I'll tell you what I thought.'
'Tell me then Pat.'
'I reckon whoever was buried there took their roses with them. Do you know what they remind me of Matthew.'
'No, what?'

'Do you remember the day we followed the river down by the caves and you said come on and look at this old house of Famine times and I remarked on the roses out the back?'

'Do you think these could be the same roses Pat, it makes you wonder doesn't it?'

The child's remains were interred in the corner of the graveyard beneath the roses. It was a simple ceremony attended to by the priest Matthew, and his friend Pat. The priest included this child in his normal religious service for the dead.

Matthew was still wondering about his ghostly experience when he remembered something he'd seen in the dentist's waiting room, as well as the fact that the receptionist was good looking. He'd go back and check. He knew he could throw more light on the situation and possibly make a date with the receptionist as well.

'Would you like to make another appointment Matthew?' she said with an inviting glint in her eye.

'No, I'm not here to see the dentist I came to see you,' he laughed. There's something I saw in one of the magazines I'd like to look at again.'

He showed her the pictures and told her a little of the story. They agreed she'd keep the magazine and meet him the next evening in a café. He considered he had pulled off a smart one by inviting her to meet him. They sat and enjoyed their coffee.

'I read about a major modelling exhibition in London,' he told her. 'Some of the names, rang a bell with me. Look at that page, that's what caught my eye.'

Major modelling exhibition from New York and London

Styles by Mary O'Shea from New York

Marion Shelten /Teresa Boyle of London

Old Style 1860   Modern Styles 1960

The Bluebell's Mystery

'It was the old style of dress, that caught my attention. There was an attractive girl dressed in a long brown overcoat. She had a woollen hat pulled down tightly on her long red hair. She was wearing a light coloured dress and laced shoes, old style. I could see that here was the girl I had seen twice in the bluebells.'

He tried to impress this story on his date, but he could not be sure she believed him, a fact that did not bother him much. He was more interested in her female attractions. Very soon he knew he would head back to the big smoke and his city girl.

He'd never forget his meeting with his ghost, or was it Mary O'Shea in the bluebells?